A King Production presents…

Who Gon Stop Me…

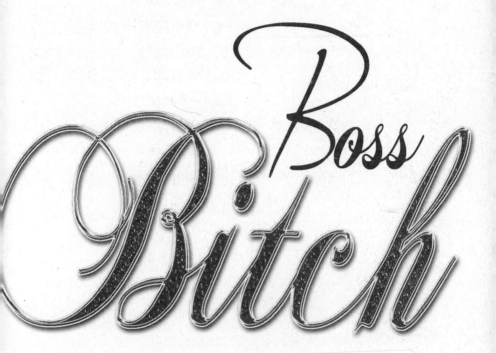

Boss Bitch

D0063727

JOY DEJA KING

This novel is a work of fiction. Any references to real people, events, establishments, or locales are intended only to give the fiction a sense of reality and authenticity. Other names, characters, and incidents occurring in the work are either the product of the author's imagination or are used fictitiously, as those fictionalized events and incidents that involve real persons. Any character that happens to share the name of a person who is an acquaintance of the author, past or present, is purely coincidental and is in no way intended to be an actual account involving that person.

ISBN 13: 978-0984332540
ISBN 10: 0984332545
Cover concept by Joy Deja King & www.MarionDesigns.com
Cover layout and graphic design by www.MarionDesigns.com
Cover Model: Joy Deja King
Typesetting: Keith Saunders
Editors: Suzy McGlown, Linda Williams and Velva White

Library of Congress Cataloging-in-Publication Data;
King, Deja Joy
Boss Bitch: a novel/by Joy Deja King
For complete Library of Congress Copyright info visit;
www.joydejaking.com

A King Production
P.O. Box 912, Collierville, TN 38027

A King Production and the above portrayal log are trademarks of
A King Production LLC

This Book is Dedicated To My:

Family, Readers and Supporters.
I LOVE you guys so much. Please believe that!!

A KING PRODUCTION

Who Gon Stop Me...

Boss Bitch

Joy Deja King

Aaliyah

They say killers are born. I believe killers are made. In life when the people you love and trust turn on you they murder your goodness. They destroy whatever innocence God gave you when you were birthed into this world. I know because I was becoming that person. After sitting in jail for over eight months, with each passing day my soul was leaving my body and I was becoming an empty vessel.

"Aaliyah, I need you to answer the question."

I paused for a moment and stared at my attorney. "What question?" I asked, not knowing or caring what he was talking about because I knew he wasn't here to give me my release papers.

"Aaliyah, we're going to trial in less than a month. I need for you to focus."

"Mr. Anderson, it's kinda hard to focus when this is what you wake up and go to sleep to everyday," I said waving my arm around, pointing to the four dreary walls that confined me.

"I understand this isn't the best accommodations but you know the judge felt with your family's financial standing you were a flight risk and wouldn't grant you bail."

That's bullshit! I was granted bail, and then they locked me back up again."

"Yes, but that was before Justina identified you as the shooter. Based on that information and the charges you're facing the judge felt you were a flight risk."

"Can you tell me something that I don't already fuckin' know? Like when the hell am I going to get out of this dump and go the hell home?"

"Aaliyah, you have to calm down. I'm doing everything I can to get you back home to your family. I have the best investigators on this case."

"They haven't come up with shit to help my case, so they can't possibly be the best."

"Unfortunately, these things can take time."

"We're both aware that time isn't something I have."

"Yes, that's why I need you to answer my questions so we can prepare for your case. Let's go over what happened at that hotel."

"We've been over this a hundred times. I've

told you everything that I remember about that night. Who you need to be grilling is Justina. She's the liar in this equation."

"I understand that but Justina is also the victim. I have to be careful how I approach her. We don't want to turn the jury against you. She was shot and in a coma so she will garner sympathy."

"Sympathy my ass. That conniving bitch is the reason I'm locked up now. She knows damn well I never pulled the trigger, although in hindsight I wish I had."

"Aaliyah, don't ever say that again. You don't know who's listening."

"Oh please, you're my attorney. That's what you get paid for, to hear me vent and hopefully get me off."

"Then I need your help. I know we've been over this many times but you never know something you might remember that can help your case."

"I've replayed that night over so many times I feel like my brain is about to explode," I said shaking my head.

"I'll tell you what, why don't we revisit this tomorrow. You have someone who has been waiting to see you, anyway."

"Someone's here to see me…who?"

"Amir."

"Amir is here?" I said standing up from my chair. "I can't believe it," I grinned.

"You're smiling, that's something I've never seen."

"Because you never give me anything to smile about."

"Before I put you back in a bad mood, let me go get Amir."

Oh fuck! I look like shit! I barely brushed my hair today. Being locked up with a bunch of broads isn't exactly a motivator to look hot. I don't want Amir to see me like this but I can't turn him away. I need him. I patted my hair down and started doing some bullshit facial exercises my mother had drilled in my head to do ever since I was a little girl. She claimed it was like giving yourself a quick facelift, which I didn't believe. But at this point I was willing to try anything if it would help me look halfway decent in front of Amir.

I looked at my reflection to see if the exercises were working but all I saw staring back at me was the same stressed and worn out face that had become a permanent fixture since being locked up. But none of that mattered when Amir walked in; he seemed to be even more handsome than I remembered if that was even possible. "I can't believe you're here."

"I'm sorry. I stayed away too long." I hadn't seen Amir in over six weeks when normally he would come see me every week. It was tearing me up inside that he'd been gone so long but what mattered was he was here with me now.

"You don't have to apologize, I'm just happy you're here," I said wrapping my arms around him. I quickly let go, knowing the guard would give me a hard time if I didn't because I could've held on to Amir forever.

"Let's sit down." I willingly followed Amir's lead wishing he would never leave. "So how are you holding up?"

"Look at me. Doesn't this face say it all?"

"You're still beautiful to me."

"Whatever," I laughed. "I appreciate you trying to make me feel better but a blatant lie isn't going to help."

"It's not a lie. You'll always be beautiful to me," Amir said, with his voice trailing off.

"You make it sound as if you're giving me some last departing words." An eerie silence fell upon us. "That was supposed to be a joke. Maybe it didn't come out right."

"Aaliyah, I wanted to tell you face-to-face

and not in some letter."

"Tell me what?"

"I can't come see you for a while."

"Why?" Amir turned away and then put his head down. "Answer me. Why can't you come see me anymore?"

"It's not forever, just for a while."

"You don't get it. Each day I'm locked up in here, feels like forever. But when you come see me, you make forever seem possible. I can't believe you're turning your back on me."

"I would never turn my back on you. But I can't turn my back on Justina either."

"Oh, so this is about Justina. She's taken everything away from me and now she's taking you away from me too." I felt the tears welling up in my eyes. I was trying to fight the burning sensation but I couldn't.

"Baby, please don't cry."

"Then make the tears stop. Don't leave me, especially when I'm down. I don't have anybody. I feel so alone."

"You're not alone. Your parents, your grand-father they're all behind you."

"My mom and dad are too busy fighting and you already know that Nico is in the middle of a war and my grandfather means well but trying to keep a family together that's divided is damn near impossible to make time for jail visits but at least he tries," I said softly as my voice trailed off.

"I promise you, I'll never abandon you."

"That's what you're doing right now."

"Justina was shot and almost died. She feels like I'm taking your side. By coming to see you, she feels like it's a slap in the face."

"Do you think I killed Sway and shot Justina?"

"Of course not. You know I don't believe that but Justina does and I have to give her my support, at least until the trial is over."

"And then what? What if I'm convicted are you going to find me guilty too and dismiss me for good."

"You won't be found guilty."

"You're only saying that to make yourself feel better for walking away. But go 'head. Poor Justina. I know how fragile she is. She needs you way more than I do. Now I know why you disappeared for the last few weeks. All the while I thought you were busy holding things down with your dad," I said sarcastically.

"Aaliyah…"

"Just stop!" I barked, cutting Amir off before

he could continue. "You've made your choice and I'll have to accept it."

"I love you both just in different ways. I want to support you but I have to help Justina too. You have to understand where I'm coming from."

"I get it. I'll be fine. One thing you're right about is that my grandfather is always behind me. As long as I have his support I can get through anything. Goodbye, Amir. I wish you well."

"Aaliyah, wait," Amir called out as I stood up and left the room. There was no reason for me to turn around and listen to whatever else he had to say. In my world you're either for me or against me, there's no in between. When Amir made the decision to stand by Justina then he was now against me, which made him my enemy.

Precious

You should never become a mother unless you're prepared to have your heart broken. I remember Ms. Duncan telling me that when I was a little girl. It seems like yesterday I was sitting in her cramped apartment in the Brooklyn projects watching her make me a hot meal as she shared what she called her words of wisdom. I barely listened to what she was saying because I was more interested in the food she was cooking. By the time my mother would drop me off, so she could go run the streets I was starving. But for some reason when she said those words they resonated with me, even as a little girl. Maybe because I wondered if one day I would break my mother's heart or would she be too high to care. Whatever the reason, here I was over thirty years later reflecting on what Ms. Duncan said and those words couldn't ring more true. My first-born child was in jail facing a first-degree murder charge and I didn't know if she would spend the rest of her life behind bars…my heart was officially broken.

"What time are you going to see Justina?" I heard Supreme ask me, taking me away from thinking about the past.

"I'm about to take a shower, get dressed and head over there."

"I have to go out of town for a couple of days but before I leave I want to go with you to speak with Justina."

"I don't think that's a good idea. Chantal was already reluctant about letting me come over. I don't want her to feel like we're trying to tag team her daughter."

"Aaliyah is going to trial in a few weeks. It's time for us to apply the pressure on Justina."

"I agree, but if we want to get answers that could help Aaliyah we have to move with caution when it comes to Justina. I know what I'm doing."

"I hope so because our daughter's life is depending on it."

"Supreme, don't you think I know how critical shit is right now," I said, lifting up from the edge of the bed. "Aaliyah is my baby. Every day she is locked up I'm locked up too."

"I apologize, that came out wrong. This shit

just got me all fucked up, Precious. I hate feeling like this, like my arms are handcuffed behind my back and I can't do shit."

"Supreme, it's gonna be ok." I stood behind Supreme and wrapped my arms around his waist. My head rested on his back and for a brief moment I felt completely connected to my husband. All the love I had for him resurfaced in an instant and then just as quickly he pushed me away.

"I can't do this with you right now, Precious," he said releasing my arms and stepping away. He walked over to the floor length windows that overlooked the custom pool with fountains, and waterfalls that streamed into a river. The water seemed to be hypnotizing Supreme because as I called out his name he ignored me.

"Supreme, you have to stop walking away from me…from us."

"You walked away a long time ago. Just because you're ready to come back doesn't mean I'm ready to have you back. Now go get dressed. You need to handle that with Justina."

I stared at Supreme for a few moments before rushing off to the bathroom. I closed the door and when I turned around I was facing myself in the mirror. With my hair up in a ballerina bun and wearing a long white silk negligee I almost appeared angelic but without sin I was not.

I slipped out of my negligee and got into the shower. When I turned on the knob and the water poured over my body it seemed as if it triggered all the pain and frustration that had been building up for the last few months to be released and I couldn't stop it. The tears flowed and the hot water washed them away but that couldn't erase the crossroads that my life was in. I was on the verge of losing my family and I was partially the blame.

My marriage was already fragile but when I began my affair with Lorenzo it was the final nail in the coffin. Although Supreme didn't know that I was seeing someone else, emotionally I had checked out but so had he. But with Aaliyah in the fucked up predicament she was in I needed Supreme's support and I was reaching out to him trying to salvage whatever was left of our marriage but I was starting to feel that I needed to admit to myself it was too late.

I closed my eyes searching for answers on how my fairytale life had turned into a nightmare. I wanted to breakdown and give in to my grief but I couldn't. I was born into a life of chaos but I beat the odds and I wouldn't fold now. My number one priority was getting Aaliyah out of jail and bringing her home. No matter what I had to do to make that happen I would and it started with Justina. Whatever was going to happen between Supreme and I would have to wait as my focus was on one problem, and crying in the shower wouldn't solve it, I decided as I turned off the water and got out. This time when I looked in the mirror I didn't see anything angelic instead I saw Precious Cummings… the fighter staring back at me.

When I arrived at Chantals' and T-Roc's house I sat in the car tapping my fingers on the steering wheel for a few minutes going over exactly how I would approach the situation. During my ride I had come up with several different scenarios but hadn't settled on one. A lot of it would depend on how forthcoming Justina was willing to be but my gut told me she was going to give me a hard time and I was prepared for that. I got out the car and walked towards the front door on a mission but I did my best to put on my game face as I rang the doorbell.

"Hello, Precious." Chantal's tone was dry and flat when she opened the door but it didn't faze me.

I wasn't expecting her to greet me with open arms. But instead of reciprocating her negative energy I played it cool and extra polite—for now.

"Chantal, thank you so much for having me over."

"You didn't leave me much of a choice." Chantal let her annoyance be known as she moved to the side to let me in.

"Where's Justina?" I asked ignoring Chantal's shade.

"She'll be down shortly."

"How are you? I know things must be difficult for you and your family right now."

"We're as good as can be expected under the circumstances. Of course this has been the most difficult for Justina."

"I can only imagine. Is T-Roc here?"

"No, he's out of town."

"When will he be back?"

"I'm not sure but it will be in time for the trial," Chantal added trying her best to get under my skin.

"Of course he will. I know he wants to be here to support his daughter," I smiled. I had never been a fan of Chantal's and it was taking all of my strength not to smack that smug look off her face but I kept my composure.

"No doubt, and speaking of our daughter here comes Justina now." I turned in the direction Chantal was looking and saw Justina coming down the stairs. I was trying to read her mood but her face and body language was telling me nothing.

"Hi, Justina, it's good to see you." Justina didn't say zilch and walked over near her mother not giving me any eye contact.

"Chantal, would you be so kind as to get me something to drink please?" I asked sitting down on the couch and crossing my legs. It was my way of letting them know I wasn't going anywhere anytime soon.

"Estelle should be down in a minute, she can get you whatever you want."

"Water would be fine, do we need to wait on the maid for me to get that?"

"If you want it then yes. That is her job."

"Of course."

"We have a lot of things to do so what exactly did you want to speak to Justina about?"

"For one I wanted to see how she was doing. Justina, I haven't seen you since you first got out of the hospital. You look great."

"Thanks."

"I'm concerned about you. It must be difficult accusing your best friend of murder and trying to take your life too." Justina remained nonresponsive and Chantal rubbed her hand as if to console her. "What did Aaliyah say to you before she shot you?"

"Huh!" Justina looked up at me for the first time and her eyes widened as if surprised by my question. "What did Aaliyah say before she pulled the trigger? I'm sure she said something…like why she wanted you dead."

"I don't remember. It all happened so fast."

"I understand. You probably went into shock."

"Yes, I did."

"So did she kill Sway first and then shoot you or did she shoot you first?"

"She shot me first, I mean Sway and then me," she said shaking her head.

"What are you doing…trying to cross examine my daughter?"

"Of course not. I'm just trying to understand what happened. Aaliyah and Justina were best friends, how did that turn into attempted murder. It doesn't make any sense. Maybe if I knew what Aaliyah said right before she tried to kill you I would get a better understanding."

"I don't remember what she said right before she shot me. But we were arguing earlier about Amir."

"As you know, your daughter was trying to get Justina's boyfriend in bed. What type of best friend is that?" Chantal snarled.

"Speaking of boyfriends, why were you in Aaliyah's boyfriend's hotel room?" I countered, ignoring Chantal's comment.

"Sway invited me."

"So what were you doing when she shot Sway?"

"I told you I don't remember. All I know is we argued about Amir. "

"So you're saying that you believe Aaliyah tried to kill you because of Amir?"

"That's exactly what she's saying," Chantal barked, answering for her daughter. "Is that so hard for you to believe?"

"Yes it is. As a matter of fact I don't believe it at all."

"Are you calling my daughter a liar?"

"Justina, isn't it true that Amir wanted to be with Aaliyah too so why would she need to get rid of you. You weren't the competition."

"You liar! Amir is committed to Justina."

"Am I lying, Justina? Why don't you tell your mother the truth?"

"I know the truth. Like mother like daughter. The same way you think you're entitled to anything you want, Precious, your spoiled daughter feels the same way. But this time Aaliyah couldn't get what she wanted. Amir chose Justina and Aaliyah couldn't handle it."

"So if it was about Amir, why kill Sway?" Silence loomed, as neither had an answer.

"Would you stop grilling my daughter?"

"Only if you stop speaking for her and let her answer the questions."

"She's my child. I have every right to speak for her."

"If she's grown enough to accuse Aaliyah of murder then she's grown enough to answer some simple questions."

"I think it's time for you to leave."

"I'll leave but trust you're not getting rid of me." I turned to Justina who was trying to maintain her sweet and innocent demeanor. "Justina, you may have your mother and father fooled and even the prosecutor but I know how to spot a snake. See you remind me a lot of someone I know. My sister Maya."

"How dare you! Justina is nothing like that twisted woman."

"But she is. Just like Maya wanted to walk in my shoes and take my life that's exactly what you're trying to do to Aaliyah but you've picked the wrong girl. Aaliyah is my daughter and I promise you'll never get away with this. Check my stats, I am not to be fucked with."

"How dare you speak to my daughter like that! You're nothing but a lowlife hoodrat."

"Chantal, shut the fuck up. I know all about your past. The fake suicide attempt, spending your entire pathetic life scheming and scamming for a come up with a man. You finally lucked up and hit the jackpot with T-Roc but you're still a miserable bitch who raised a miserable daughter. So call me a hoodrat if you like but this Brooklyn Bitch is going to bring your daughter down and if you get in my way I'll take yo' ass down too. Now I'm leaving," I spit, grabbing my purse and making an exit.

After I slammed the door, I turned around tempted to go back inside and slaughter mother and daughter but I knew this wasn't the time for me to be sitting in a cell next to Aaliyah. What I also knew was not only was Justina lying but I believed she knew a lot more than what she was letting on, now I had to figure out how to prove it. As I got in my car I felt my phone vibrating and it was Quentin.

"Hey, Quentin, what's going on?"

"Are you home? I wanted to stop by and talk to you about something important."

"Actually I'm leaving Chantal's house. I just had an interesting conversation with her and Justina."

"Don't they live near Nico?"

"Yes, only about fifteen minutes away."

"Then meet me at Nico's place. I can discuss this with both of you at the same time."

"I'm on my way." Before I hung up with Quentin I saw Lorenzo beeping on the other line but I ignored his call. Part of me wanted to hear his voice because I knew he would say all the right things to make me feel better but that feeling would only last for a moment. Since beginning my affair with Lorenzo almost a year ago he had become my ultimate high and also represented how low things had become in my life. With all the chaos surrounding me right now Lorenzo would only be a distraction I didn't need.

Between thinking about Lorenzo, replaying the conversation I had with Chantal and Justina, and wondering what the hell Quentin had to talk to us about, I seemed to arrive at Nico's estate in a matter of a few minutes. When I turned onto Frick Drive, the first thing I noticed when I pulled up was there wasn't a security guard posted in the front and the gate was open. I figured they were in the middle of a shift change and I continued on the long spiral heated stone driveway until I reached the colonial styled mansion. Nico and Quentin were standing out front when I arrived so I wasted no time walking towards them.

"I hope you all haven't started without me because I'll be pissed if you have." I gave a slight smile, letting them know I wasn't completely serious but a tad bit.

"No, we were discussing some other business until you got here. But I must say that was rather fast," Quentin commented after eyeing his watch.

"You know I like to speed plus I was anxious to find out what you needed to tell us." I paused and looked at Nico realizing I hadn't spoken. "How are you?"

"I've seen much better days that's for sure."

"Besides everything that's going on with our daughter is there something else bothering you?"

"Business is extremely shaky right now but

21

we can talk about that later. I want to hear what Quentin has to tell us, but let's go inside. It looks like it's about to start pouring down," Nico commented, looking up at the dark clouds that were forming in the sky.

"A little water has never hurt anybody," I giggled, following Nico and Quentin inside. Entering Nico's crib always felt like the first time to me and my initial thought was *this place is too fuckin' beautiful for him to be living here alone*. Nico lived in the nation's wealthiest zip code at least according to the Forbes list. Whether true or not, his 20,000 sq. ft. American masterpiece was the quintessential Alpine estate. We ended up in the banquet-sized dining room and before we even sat down Quentin cut right to it.

"Nico, remember when I told you I had a close associate investigating some leads into Aaliyah's case?" Nico nodded his head. "Well he came back with some very interesting information."

"Like what?" I quickly asked. Feeling some sort of hope an emotion that had been eluding me for some time.

"Since we know Aaliyah wasn't the shooter, whoever was, got into that hotel room without damaging the door. I figured nobody let them in so they must've had a key. That means they had some inside help. I had him run a check on everybody that was working that night."

"And what did he come up with?" Nico questioned, leaning forward on the black marble table.

"Three people piqued his interest but one person stood out in particular."

"Why?"

"After checking her bank records and speaking to a few people that live in her building, she went from barely being able to pay her rent each month to having new furniture delivered to her apartment, wearing designer clothes, shoes, purses, and for the last four months sizeable deposits being made into her bank account."

"Get the fuck outta here! Does she still work for the hotel?" I asked as my heart raced believing that finally we found a lead.

"She quit a little over a month ago. Not that she's needed the job. I believe she was trying to play it safe not to raise suspicion. But now after all these months have passed she feels it's no longer necessary to keep up the charade."

"So what is she doing now?"

"My guy has been on her day and night for the last week. He wanted to see if she would meet up with whoever is involved with the shooting. But no such luck. All she's been doing is shopping, partying and going out to eat with her friends. She's living her life like she ain't got a care in the world."

"All while Aaliyah has been sittin' in jail for months. Yeah, somebody's paying that ass off real good for the service she provided and it ain't no sugar daddy. If we find out who that is I guarantee it'll point to our shooter."

"Were you able to trace the account to see where the money is coming from?" Nico wanted to know and so did I.

"Whoever is making the deposits is using cash and there's no way for us to trace. We've checked her cell phone records and if she's in contact with the person they using bullshit or throwaway phones to talk."

"So what are we gonna do? Aaliyah goes to trial in a few weeks and shit is critical right now! I would say let's take this information to the cops but I know they'll fuck this shit up."

"You damn right! They have it out for Aaliyah. They believe she's the perp and they ain't tryna hear nothing else."

"Yeah, thanks to Justina and after my conver- sation with her today she has no plans to change her story. I swear I wanted to fuck her and her mother up today."

"I still don't understand how Justina could lie on Aaliyah like that. They were best friends. They practically grew up together. You know how many times she has spent the night at this house with her. I mean damn. I treated that girl like she was my own daughter and for her to turn on Aaliyah… I'll never understand."

"Nico, its called jealousy and it makes people do some fucked up shit. Justina has always been jealous of Aaliyah but that Amir situation just sent her over the edge. The one thing she felt she had that Aaliyah didn't was Amir. When she found out they had feelings for each other all bets were off. Somehow in her twisted mind she thought if she blamed the shooting on Aaliyah she could get rid of the competition for good and Amir would be all hers."

"You telling me that she's ruining our daughter's life for some boyfriend shit? These young kids today, I just don't understand." Nico shook his head in disbelief.

"Listen," Quentin spoke up wanting our full attention. "I think it's time we confront this woman. I think we can all agree the cops won't be any benefit to us right now. Technically this woman is an accessory to murder. She's not going to willingly admit to anything because she could be facing a shit load of time behind bars. But we just need to let her know we're not interested in turning her in. All we want is a name and we'll handle it from there and leave her out of it."

"Sounds like a plan. Where does she live?" I waited for Quentin to give us the address and I put it in my phone. "You all ready to go now?"

"Hold up. My guy is keeping tabs on her and right now she's not home. He's going to call me as soon as she's on her way back to her apartment. We want to catch her when she's alone. As soon as he calls me, I'll call the two of you so be on alert."

"Let's do this. I'm headed to Manhattan right now. I got the address, I'll be sitting right in front of her apartment building until you tell me we can go in," I said, grabbing my car keys off the table. I was anxious to confront the woman and couldn't get across the bridge fast enough.

"I'm with you, let's go," Nico chimed in. "Precious, you can leave your car here and ride with me."

"That'll work."

"I should be calling you within the next hour

or so with an update. Then I'll head into the city and meet up with you at the apartment."

"We'll be waiting for your call, but Quentin, the moment you hear anything hit us up. I want to be aware of everything that's going on. I wish you would've came to us sooner with this information."

"Nico, I didn't want to get you all's hopes up if this turned out to be a dead end. I wanted my investigator to get some sort of concrete proof that this woman was somehow involved before bringing it to you and Precious and that took time."

"I get that but I could've had some of my security men following her too. Or checking on some things your man might've missed." Nico paused in the middle of the all white marble foyer locking eyes with Quentin before he continued to vent, "I know you mean well but this is my daughter and this is her life we're talking about. She's been sitting in a jail cell for months and if somebody can get her the fuck out then we need as many people on it as possible. I got plenty of security men that need some shit to do," Nico popped as he opened the front door, stepping to the side to let me out.

"Speaking of security, I noticed you didn't have any at the front gate when I was pulling in."

"You sure about that?" Nico asked with a

quizzical stare. "So how did you get in then?"

"The gates were open?"

"Get the fuck outta here! You telling me these muthafuckas bullshitting on the job....slack ass niggas."

"I thought maybe they were between shifts."

"Nah, two men supposed to be posted up at the gate at all times," Nico barked looking down at his watch and then getting on his cell phone. "Hold up, let me see what these clowns are doing before we leave."

"Precious, I'll be in touch shortly. Let me go handle a couple things before I meet you all in the city," Quentin said, before heading to his car. But right as he turned to leave it was as if a hail of bullets replaced the rain falling from the sky.

It seemed everything went blank in less than thirty seconds. Within a few moments I saw two Suburban trucks pull up with men wearing black ski mask spraying shit up. Normally in these situations time would seem to stand still as the chaos erupts around you because you're in shock but shit was moving extra fast like I was pressing the expedite button. It was like *boom* the sounds of machine guns were filling the air, then *boom* Nico grabbed a gun from the back of his slacks and some of his security men came running out the house blasting off and then *boom* I was out cold.

The next thing I remember was my chest feeling weighted down and I was having difficulty breathing. Then I felt this excruciating pain on the back of my head, as my eyes tried to open. But my eyelids were heavy and kept shutting back close as I was fighting to open them up. The rain was coming down on me and between the thunder and lightning I heard a faint voice speaking but all I could understand was they were calling out my name. As I struggled to gain some sort of balance I kept thinking I must've been shot, that's why my chest felt like a ton of bricks was weighing down on it.

"Precious, are you okay?" I heard the voice call out again but this time I recognized it, it was Nico. I tried to mumble something but it didn't come out as clearly as I hoped. I tried to relax my mind and body and I finally managed to keep my eyes open for longer than a second and I was horrified by what I saw. Quentin, my father was the heavy load I felt on my chest. His body was on top of mine and he wasn't moving. I could see the blood pouring down around us mixed with rain.

"Precious, stay calm. The paramedics will be

here any minute. Are you hurt…were you shot?"

"I think I'm okay. What about Quentin?'

"He's not responding but I can feel a slight pulse." To my relief I could hear the ambulance getting closer. There was still a chance to save Quentin and I was praying they were able to do that. Nico held my hand as my eyes began to close again. My head was throbbing and the pain was excruciating. Before I could say another word it was lights out for me.

Aaliyah

As I sat in my jail cell I kept rereading the last letter Amir had wrote me. I was looking for clues that he was ready to abandon me like he did a couple of days ago but there were none. The letter was upbeat, sweet and full of hope, something he took away from me in a matter of one conversation.

"What you reading?" my cellmate asked me as she was getting her stuff together.

"Oh nothing," I said balling up the letter and tossing it on the floor. "I know you're excited to be getting the hell out of here," I smiled, wanting to get Amir off my mind if only for a few minutes.

"You know it, girly! I'm so over this dump. I can't wait to get back on these streets where I belong and make that money."

"Well I hope you have a plan."

"Of course! I already got shit lined up. My people got me setup lovely," she bragged.

"Good for you! I want things to work out 'cause I def don't want to see you back up in here."

"Hell nah! I did my time and learned what not to do to avoid stepping foot back up in this joint."

"Yeah, you lucky."

"You gon' be lucky too. Just wait and see."

"I hope you right, Peaches, 'cause shit is looking all sorts of shaky for me."

"I know, Ma, but when things seem to be at their worse that's when you have to be at your strongest."

"So true and trust me I'm working on it."

"Plus, I need you to get out so you can help me run this empire I'm building," Peaches beamed.

"Empire? Girl, you only twenty-one, what type of empire you building?"

"The same kind your daddy got and I ain't talking 'bout music." We both laughed for a sec before curiosity got the best of me.

"You must have a serious connect if you ready to build an empire."

"You have no idea. But like I said I want you right next to me as a partner."

"You want me as your partner?" I pointed to myself in disbelief.

"Why you acting so surprised? Yes, I want you," she pointed back. "What's so hard to believe about that?"

"For one, I don't think I'll be getting out anytime soon, and even if I did, I think we're both a little young to be trying to build an empire in that particular line of work."

"You're underestimating your capabilities. I saw how you turned into a beast trying to protect me and I'll never forget that shit."

I knew exactly what situation Peaches was talking about and that shit seemed like it happened yesterday. My mind thought back to when it all went down. Peaches had been my cellmate from the start but she never said shit to me. At first I thought she couldn't talk. After I had been there for a couple of weeks she started saying a few words to me but not much. I figured she was shy. She kept to herself, would read, she would eat by herself and didn't bother nobody. I was cool with a couple of the inmates, nothing major but everybody knew who I was because my case was so high profile so nobody really fucked with me but the same couldn't be said for Peaches. This one little click of chicks had it in for her bad. They started off doing stupid silly shit, like tripping her so she would drop her tray of food. Or hanging up the phone when she was on a call but then shit started escalating. One day when she was in the shower they tried to jump her and that shit didn't sit right with me and I wouldn't allow it. I was able to let the other bullshit slide but when you're locked up and you see a tiny girl that don't bother nobody about to get her ass beat down it does something to you.

"Why are you guys doing this!" I heard a voice scream out as I was getting dressed. It was coming from the shower area I just left. Then I heard a gang of girls laughing and joking, a few seconds later I heard that same voice crying out pleading for them to stop. I looked around and all the women kept doing their own thing as if they didn't hear the girl pleading for help. I went back to the shower to see what was going on and it was four girls surrounding one girl who was on the shower floor using her hands trying to cover her face and body as they kept kicking her. As I stepped closer I realized it was my cellmate. She looked like a wounded puppy surrounded by wolves. I had to do something.

"That's enough," I called out. At first nobody acknowledged me. I wasn't sure if they were purposely trying to ignore me or because of all the commotion they simply didn't hear me so this time I walked closer and spoke even louder. "I said that's enough!" This time they all stopped and turned to see who was interrupting them.

"If you know what's good for you, you're turn around and get the fuck outta here 'cause this ain't none of your business," the leader of the pack warned me. At that moment I knew I could do one or two things; walk away and let the innocent girl be beat and possibly raped or I could just start swinging. I had been locked up long enough to know there was no negotiating with words. Inmates saw that as a sign of weakness. So without saying another word, I just walked up to the woman that threatened me and punched her in the mouth with all the strength I had. She hit the floor so fast and hard the other three girls were in shock.

"Bitch, are you crazy!" One of the girls finally said so I grabbed her by her hair and punched her in the mouth too and then I slammed her head down on the shower floor. Then the last two girls standing decided it was do or die so they knocked me down and jumped on top of me. By this time my adrenaline was pumping to the next level. I wasn't even scared I had no fear. I was swinging my fist and kicking my legs. They was getting a few punches in but I felt no pain. Then the other two girls I had laid down got back their composure and came at me too. I guess with all this going down Peaches grew a backbone and decided to become my hero. She came back swinging, and I mean literally. She got a hold of a broom and started cracking backs with it. Those hoes started scrambling like cockroaches.

"Are you okay?"

"I'm fine," I said wiping the blood from the side of my mouth.

"Why did you help me?"

"Because that shit they was doing to you was fucked up."

"I can't believe you stood up for me like that. You got a lot of heart. I'll never forget what you done for me and one day I'll return the favor. That's a promise." From that day on Peaches and me became super cool.

"Just because I protected you doesn't mean I'm equipped to be your partner in building an empire."

"I told you then and I'm telling you now… you got heart. That's the most important thing you need to be a great partner. Plus this shit run through your blood, you were built for this."

"You sound so confident in me."

"Because I am. I've watched how you moved since you've been here. You might come from privilege but you're a fighter and you stand up for what you believe in. I respect you, Aaliyah. And when you get out I'll be waiting for you."

"You might be waiting for a long time like twenty-five to life."

"I don't think so but no matter how long it takes, I'll be here. We're family now and family takes care of each other."

"Aaliyah, your attorney is here to see you," I heard the guard call out interrupting my conversation with Peaches.

"Go 'head, I'll be in touch," Peaches said, giving me a hug before I left. "Remember when things seem to be at their worse you have to get stronger." I smiled at Peaches and left. She was right, during these last few months we had become like family and I was going to miss her. But there was no time for me to think about that. I had a murder charge to fight and there was no doubt in my mind my attorney was here to discuss just that.

"Good afternoon, Mr. Anderson. I can't say that I'm surprised to see you again so soon, especially since my trial starts in a few short weeks. I've been writing things down like you suggested but I still haven't come up with anything new."

"Have a seat, Aaliyah."

"I know I'm not being exactly helpful but I really don't need the somber face."

"There's no easy way for me to tell you this so I'm just going to say it."

"What's going on?" I kept standing up waiting for my attorney to answer me.

"Sit down."

"I don't want to sit down. I want you to tell me what's going on."

"Your mother is in the hospital with a minor concussion and she'll be fine but your grandfather is in critical condition." My legs buckled up underneath me and I was forced to sit down in my chair or I would've fallen down.

"What happened?"

"He was shot. From what Nico told me, they were ambushed. Your grandfather was protecting your mother and took a bullet."

"Is he gonna make it?"

"I don't know. It's serious."

"Do they know who did it?"

"I don't believe so. I know with all you're

going through, this is the last thing you were expecting but I need you to stay focused on the case."

"How can I do that with my mother in the hospital and my grandfather in critical condition. When did this happen?"

"Yesterday afternoon. I found out last night."

"Why is my life so fucked up," I said, shaking my head. "If my grandfather doesn't make it, I don't know what I'll do. All my life, he's the only person that has stood by my side and never judges me, no matter how many times I've screwed up. I can't lose him." I had been wearing such a tough exterior while being locked up but with this news I couldn't hold in my pain. I cried and I couldn't stop crying. When Amir turned his back on me, knowing I had my grandfather made it bearable but now, I wasn't sure what I would do.

"Aaliyah, your grandfather wouldn't want you to give up. I've known him for many years and he's a great man. If you have any chance of getting out of jail, you have to pull it together. If you can't do it for yourself then do it for your grandfather."

I heard what Mr. Anderson was saying but my mind was someplace else. For just a moment I wanted to go back to a time where I was happy and life seemed beautiful and I didn't have a care in the world. I was six-years-old and the sun was bright and the sky was clear. My grandfather was pushing me on the swing and I kept yelling that I wanted to go higher and higher. I was giggling and laughing. I never appreciated that moment of pure happiness until right now. I would give anything to have it back but I couldn't because there was no turning back time.

Precious

"What the fuck happened?" I kept asking as I slightly opened my eyes. When I turned to see who was standing over me, I could barely move my head. If I did, it felt as if someone was bashing me with a baseball bat. The pain was excruciating.

"Don't try to move," I heard a familiar voice say. As my vision became clear I recognized the face to be Lorenzo.

"Where am I?"

"You're at the hospital."

"The hospital?" I asked feeling confused. "Why, what happened?"

"I don't know all the details but from what Genesis told me, you, Quentin and Nico were ambushed at his house. When Quentin was trying to protect you, the back of your head hit a stone or something and it knocked you out cold. The doctor said you have a concussion. You don't remember anything?"

"It's all so blurry. I remember all of us walking out the house…oh gosh," I said putting my hand on my head as the throbbing pain kicked back in.

"Are you okay?" Lorenzo wanted to know as he took my other hand and held it. "Do you want me to get the doctor?"

"Not right now. The pain is going in and out. I'm okay. So what about Nico and Quentin, are they fine?"

"Nico is fine but Quentin…" Lorenzo paused and didn't say anything.

"What about Quentin?"

"I don't want you getting yourself worked up."

"Lorenzo, tell me what happened to Quentin. He's not dead is he?" I asked as my voice trembled. I was afraid to ask the question but I wanted to know.

"No he isn't dead but it's not looking good. He had to get surgery yesterday to remove the bullet and is in ICU."

"This all happened yesterday? Who has my son?"

"Yes this all went down yesterday. But your son is fine. From what I heard, Nico called Supreme and told him what happened. He's out of town but he's on his way back so he had his parents go stay with Xavier."

"Oh good. I still can't believe Quentin might not make it. Because he was trying to save my life he might lose his. I felt like crying but my head was hurting too bad so all I could do was shed tears on the inside for my father.

"Quentin is a soldier; we're all hoping he pulls through. But I need you to try and stay calm. I'ma go get the doctor."

"Lorenzo," I called out as he was walking out. "Thank you for being here when I woke up."

"There was no other place I wanted to be." Before I could get lost in my thoughts Genesis came in.

"Genesis, is Quentin any better?"

"Nico is in the ICU now talking to his doctor. How are you?"

"Alive, which is a blessing. What's going on, why were we ambushed and by who?"

"A war has been brewing for a few months now but we weren't prepared for this. If we lose Quentin behind this bullshit I might be done with this game for good but not before I murk everybody that had something to do with this."

"Does the killing ever stop? I'm so tired of being surrounded by death. It's like I can't escape it."

"Precious, I'm so sorry you've gotten caught

up in the middle of this. This isn't your war to fight but it's always the innocent that gets hurt."

"You don't have to apologize to me, Genesis, I might be the victim in this particular situation but you and I both know I'm far from innocent. Right now I'm worried about Quentin. And what about you, Nico and Lorenzo?"

"We've beefed up security."

"I hate this is happening. I can't believe I'm saying this but maybe it's good Aaliyah is in jail. She might be safer there. You know when a war breaks out, one of the first things the enemy does is go after loved ones. Aaliyah is Nico's only living relative, she would no doubt be a prime target."

"I promise you whether Aaliyah is in or out of jail we will not let anything happen to her. We'll protect her, Precious. I don't want you to worry about that."

"Genesis, I've been in the game for a very long time and honestly I don't believe I've ever left it. And one thing we both know, is that's a promise that is impossible to keep."

"Then I'll die trying."

Before I could respond to Genesis, we both turned towards the door when we heard Nico come in. "Precious, you're awake."

"Yes, how's Quentin?"

"The surgery went well but the doctor doesn't know if or when Quentin will wake up. All of us just have to pray that he makes it."

"He has to make it. You know how close Aaliyah is to Quentin. She's going to go crazy when she finds out what happened to him."

"I know. But that's why we have to get her out so she can be with her grandfather."

"Get her out…yes there might be a way to get Aaliyah out! It's coming back to me now. Before we walked out the house Quentin was telling us about a way we might be able to clear Aaliyah's name and get her out of jail. Nico, we have to go," I said pulling the blanket off of me and trying to get out of bed.

"Precious, what are you doing?" Genesis said in concern, grabbing my arm.

"You're not going anywhere but back in the bed," Nico demanded, coming around to the other side to help hold me up. I was light headed and felt I could fall over any minute.

"But we have to follow up on that lead."

"Mrs. Mills, what are you doing out of the bed?" I looked up at the doctor who was standing in front of Lorenzo. My eyes darted to his and I could see he wanted to ask me the same thing but remained quiet because Nico was in the room.

"I need to get dressed and check out. I have some very important things I need to take care of."

"They'll have to wait. You suffered a severe concussion and you're lucky you can stand up at all. You need to stay in the hospital and be monitored for at least the next couple of days."

"That's impossible!"

"This isn't up for negotiation. If you leave this hospital right now, there is a chance you can walk out of here and die. We need to wait until all your test have come back and make sure there isn't any permanent damage to your brain."

"Precious, please listen to the doctor," Genesis pleaded. "You won't be any good to Aaliyah if you're dead."

"Fine. But Nico don't make any moves without me," I huffed.

"Nico, let me talk to you for a minute in the hallway," Genesis said after they finished helping me get back in the bed.

"Sure, we'll be back in a minute, Precious. Try not to take your frustration out on the good doctor while we're gone."

"Funny," I countered as the doctor began

checking my vitals.

"You know everybody is right. I know you want to help your daughter but you have to get better first."

"Lorenzo, I'm not in the mood for a lecture."

"I'm not trying to give you one. I just want you to get better. You need to get some rest and I know you have some calls to make so I'll be going."

"Wait, are you coming back?"

"Only if you want me to."

"I'll call you later." Lorenzo nodded his head and left. I knew when he made the statement about making calls he was referring to Supreme. But he was my husband and of course I had to speak to him.

"Mrs. Mills, everything seems to be fine but you need to get some rest. I'll be back later to check up on you but of course if you need anything a nurse will be right in."

"Thank you but I'm sure I'll be fine. Before you go can you please hand me my purse off the chair?"

"Sure." After the doctor handed me my purse and left I reached inside for my phone.

"Fuck, my battery is dead." I decided to try

and call Supreme from the phone in my room but I doubted he would answer since he wouldn't recognize the number. His phone rang several times before going to voicemail. I left him a detailed message asking him to call me back as soon as possible.

"The doctor said everything is looking good," Nico said when him and Genesis came back in my room.

"Yeah, does that mean I'll be able to get the hell out of here tomorrow?"

"Precious, I know this is asking a lot but please try to relax."

"You want to help me to relax, get me a damn charger for my phone."

"You got an iPhone right?"

"Yes, I'll get that for you. But so you know I did call Supreme and Xavier is with his grandparents."

"Thanks I appreciate that," I smiled not letting Nico know Lorenzo already told me.

"Do you need anything else," Genesis asked. "Food, magazines, books?"

"Thanks for asking but I'm good for now."

"We're going to have a security guard posted outside your room at all times so don't worry you're protected."

"Thank you, Genesis. I'll let you"…before I could finish my sentence the phone started ringing. "This is probably Supreme calling me back."

"You take your call, we'll be back later."

"Thank you both for everything," I said, before answering the phone. "Hello."

"How are you?"

"Pretty good. Are you back?"

"Not yet."

"What are you waiting on?"

"This business I had to handle is taking a lot longer than I expected. But Xavier is good. He's with my parents."

"What about me?"

"You said you're good."

"I guess it's crazy for me to think my husband would want to be with me while I'm in the hospital."

"Precious, even if I was in town there's nothing I could do for you anyway."

"How about give me your support."

"You have my support. How is Quentin?"

"His surgery went fine but he's in ICU. I'm worried about him."

"So am I. Quentin is a good man. He didn't deserve that."

"I know. So you'll be back tonight?"

"Hopefully."

"Hopefully! Supreme, there is so much going on right now. I need you."

"Precious, I'm trying to handle some very important business. As soon as I'm done I'll be home. I'll call you later on to check on you. I love you…bye."

"Bye." When I hung up the phone all I felt was despair. My daughter was in jail, my father was barely clinging on to his life and my husband seemed to be slipping away more and more each day. I decided to call Xavier because I knew hearing his sweet voice would make this dark cloud over me disappear. But right as I was dialing the number the devil herself stepped in my room.

"Precious, I'm so glad to see you're doing better. I was concerned."

"Maya, what the hell are you doing here and why in the hell did the security let you in my room?"

"I'm your sister. Of course they let me see you, we're family."

"Can't you go torture somebody else…I can't deal with you right now."

"I'm not here to torture you. I was devastated to hear that not only was my sister in the hospital but my father was shot and is in critical condition. We need to put our differences aside and come together right now. Our father would want that."

"Maya, I'm just starting to get over my concussion if I have to continue this conversation with you I might end up in a permanent coma."

"You shouldn't joke about something so serious, Precious."

"I'm not joking, I'm being very serious. I'm supposed to be resting and you bring out the very worse in me. So if you're truly concerned about my well-being then leave."

"Our father would want me to be here with you…you know to show my support. Speaking of support where is Supreme?"

"Don't worry about where Supreme is at. None of us is any of your business."

"I understand why you're being so hostile. Because of you our father may die. He was trying to protect the daughter who constantly turned him away. That must be a heavy burden to carry. The guilt must be eating you up," Maya stated sliding her hair behind her ear. The other side of her mid length bob slightly covered her eye but I could still see the evil lurking. I looked down at her nude pumps with cream slacks and a baby powder blue blouse. She stood there casually dangling her crocodile clutch purse. She even had on a string of pearls to compliment her look. I couldn't lie her entire appearance was the replica of what an upstanding woman about her business would look like and that shit was scary because the bitch was crazy. Maya was the perfect example of why you should never judge a book by its cover.

"The only thing eating me up is that we're in a hospital and I can't muster up enough strength to get up and whoop yo' ass up out my room. But I'm cool wit' that because I'll see you again and your presence is motivating me to get well soon."

"You do that, my dear sister because with your husband nowhere around and your daughter about to spend the rest of her life in prison, Xavier needs somebody to care for him. It's such a shame how you used to have it all but now look at you. And to think I used to want to be you. All I can do is shake my head, oh how the mighty has fallen."

"I see age hasn't taught you nothing because the harder I fall the stronger I rise. Now get the fuck out my room."

"Get well soon, Precious," Maya smirked before making her exit. When Maya left I sat there for a few minutes regretting that I didn't allow

Supreme to have someone kill her or better yet that I didn't kill her myself. I wanted Quentin to live but at that moment I promised myself that if he didn't pull through I would see to it that Maya died right along with him.

Aaliyah

As I stood waiting for the police officers to escort me into the courtroom the fear that I had buried for the last few months swallowed me. The day had finally arrived, the beginning of my trial. I was facing First Degree Murder charges and Attempted Murder. For some reason I didn't believe this day would ever come I guess because I didn't want to believe it.

"Let's go," I heard the officer say, grabbing my arm. When I entered the courtroom even though the air conditioner was blasting I could feel sweat surfacing on my forehead. I felt like I was in a sauna. Luckily my hair was pulled back in a bun or it would've been sticking to my face.

"Are you okay?" my attorney asked me when I reached the table where I would be sitting for the duration of the trial. "Sit down, you look like you're about to pass out," he said, pouring me a glass of water. "Drink this." Mr. Anderson practically had to shove the glass in my hand because drinking water was the last thing on my mind. There were only two things I kept thinking about: spending the rest of my life behind bars and my grandfather dying.

"I'm fine," I finally said as my voice cracked. I took a few sips of water and rubbed my sweaty palms together. I looked around and saw my mother and father sitting together. A few seats behind them I saw Nico and Genesis sitting together. They all gave me warm smiles trying to reassure me that everything would be ok. Then my eyes darted to the other side of the courtroom and I saw Justina. When I thought my heart couldn't be crushed any further, a painful knot in the pit of my stomach formed when I saw Amir sitting next to Justina. Our eyes locked for a few seconds and then I turned away as I didn't want him to see the single tear that had escaped my eye. I tried to discreetly wipe it away but wiping away the tear couldn't wipe away the pain.

"Please rise." I heard the officer say when the judge presiding over my trial entered the courtroom. My legs felt so weak when I stood up I was afraid they would buckle up under me. I held on to the table to maintain my balance. The room seemed to be spinning and I was relieved when we were able to sit back down. My mind had zoned out. I was no longer in the building. Instead of listening to opening arguments I reflected on what my mother said to me yesterday when she visited me in jail. She promised me that I would beat this case and be able to finally come home. My mother seemed so sincere when she rubbed the side of my face, looked me in the eyes and told me that. I looked down at the taupe colored dress she brought for me to wear. With the bun and the conservative dress I resembled a young and innocent schoolteacher. But all of us knew it was going to take much more than a pure as the driven snow image to beat these charges, it would take a miracle.

I looked over at the jury that consisted of five women and seven men and the two alternates. When they were sworn in I wondered would these be the people that would give me back my freedom or have me locked up for the rest of my life. My attorney told me the trial shouldn't last longer than a week, two weeks max but I knew it would be the longest week or two of my life.

"Your Honor, the first witness we'll be calling is Justina Morgan." When I heard the prosecutor say that it got my attention and snapped me out of my daydreaming. As scared as I was I needed to focus.

"I had no idea Justina was the first witness," I whispered to my attorney.

"Clearly the prosecutor is trying to set the stage early."

"What do you mean?"

"She wants to immediately imprint in the minds of the jurors that you are the killer. So either they believe they have a very strong case or a weak one."

Fuck...Fuck...Fuck is all I kept screaming to myself. I watched in disgust as Justina's pathetic ass strolled to the witness stand with her head slightly down like she was a victim. Her hair was blown out straight hanging slightly past her shoulders. She had that, I really don't have that much makeup on look but in all actuality her face was beat to perfection in very natural tones. Her pink blouse and pencil skirt with heels gave off young but sophisticated. Justina must've had her mother dress her because the outfit had Chantal written all over it. Yeah, these heifers were no doubt out to fry me and came dressed for the occasion.

"Would you please state your name for the courtroom," the prosecutor stated after Justina was sworn in. *Damn, we done heard her name a few times we know who the fuck she is*, I said to myself, trying not to let the repulsion I had for Justina show on my face. My attorney had already warned me not to wear my emotions on my face unless it's one of innocence. The thing was, I knew I was innocent so every face I made still made that true but I guess jurors didn't see it that way.

"Justina Morgan."

"Justina how do you know the defendant?"

"We grew up together. We used to be best friends before I was shot." I caught the jurors glance their eyes towards me and tried to sit up a little extra straighter. I felt those sweat beads about to accumulate again so I quickly took another sip of water. My attorney gently touched my hand letting me know it would be ok.

"Justina, can you walk us through the events that led up to the shooting on July 15th."

"It all started when I caught Aaliyah trying to have sex with my boyfriend."

"Objection, your Honor," Mr. Anderson swiftly stood up and barked. Now I understood exactly why she was the prosecutor's first witness. They wanted to assassinate my character before jurors even had a chance to hear the evidence. By the time we put on a defense in their mind I would already be guilty. I sat in horror for the next hour listening to Justina give her version of the play by play of that night. Most of what she said was completely one sided. She was the loyal sweet girlfriend who was backstabbed by her conniving best friend. The way she described what went down she almost had me not liking myself until I realized it was all lies.

"I have no further questions," the prosecutor said, sitting back down. I let out a sigh of relief. I was tired of hearing Justina spew her lies so eloquently. I was now praying that my attorney could do some damage control but I wasn't optimistic. The scary part was that Justina really was a victim, which didn't help my cause. Somebody did put a bullet through her but the problem was it wasn't me. But how did my attorney prove that Justina was lying without attacking her since she was a victim.

"Why were you in Sway Stone's hotel room in the middle of the night?" that was the first question out of my attorney's mouth. I was surprised but pleased he took that route. He completely bypassed that love triangle bullshit that Justina conveniently threw out there to make me look like shit.

"I already answered that question," Justina responded in a sugary tone.

"Actually you didn't. So can you explain that to me now." When I thought about it, my attorney was right, the prosecutor never asked her and she never explained. They just conveniently jumped to the hotel room without explaining how she ended. up there.

"Yeah, expose all her hoe shit," I mumbled under my breath as I waited for Justina to give her explanation. Justina looked over at the prosecutor's table as if she expected for her to object but instead she leaned forward with her glasses perched on the tip of her nose as if anxiously awaiting the answer too.

"He invited me there," she answered clearing her throat.

"Mr. Stone invited you there for what reason?'

"He wanted to talk."

"About?"

"He was interested in pursuing a relationship with me as he had grown tired of dealing with Aaliyah."

"I see. So it was a romantic conversation?"

"Yes. Sway Stone was romantically interested in me."

"Was the feeling mutual?"

"No I still wanted to work on my relationship

with Amir."

"But you were still at Mr. Stone's hotel room in the middle of the night."

"Objection Your Honor, this is argumentative," the prosecutor barked.

"Strike that, I'll move on to my next question, Your Honor. Justina, after Sway made his intentions known to you what happened next?"

"That's when Aaliyah showed up. Sway asked her to leave because he told her he wanted to be with me and he was done with her. "

"Didn't Aaliyah show up because Mr. Stone left the room key at the front desk for her?"

"Yes, but that was only because he wanted to break things off with her, face to face."

"And that's what he did when she arrived?"

"Yes, as soon as she arrived they started arguing because he said he was done with her."

"But you just testified that when Aaliyah got to the hotel the two of you were arguing about Amir, which one is it?"

"It's both."

"It can't be both. It's called a sequence to events. Did Aaliyah argue with you first or did she argue with Mr. Stone?'

"She argued with me first and then Sway,"

Justina huffed.

"So after the two of you argued about Amir, that's when Mr. Stone then told Aaliyah he wanted to be with you and not her?"

"Yes. She couldn't take the fact that after she threw herself at Amir he didn't want her and now Sway didn't want her. They both wanted me."

"Stop lying! You came to that hotel room and threw yourself at Sway and he still turned you down!" I yelled out as if I wasn't in a courtroom full of people.

"Aaliyah, sit down," Mr. Anderson directed me, coming towards the table.

"Justina, why don't you tell the truth for once and stop lying! This is my life we're talking about," I continued, sick of this deceitful bitch playing with my livelihood.

"Control your client, or she will be escorted out of this courtroom, immediately," the judge threatened as he banged his gavel up and down.

"Aaliyah, get a hold of yourself. Are you trying to spend the rest of your life in jail?" Mr. Anderson said in a low but furious voice. "I understand you're upset but let me handle the witness. You need to sit there and just listen. Can you do that?"

"Yes," I answered still ready to give Justina

the riot act.

"Are you sure because if not then you need to leave. You're no good for me if you can't sit there quietly."

"I'm sure."

"Are you able to get your client under control because outburst like that won't be tolerated in my courtroom."

"Yes, Your Honor and we apologize. It will not happen again."

"It better not or your client will be in even more trouble than she already is." I caught the smirk on Justina's face and I swear I had to call on the good Lord to give me strength. I turned around and I caught my mother mouth the words *be strong* to me. I turned back around and shook my head. There was a part of me that wanted to believe that maybe the injury Justina sustained had messed up her memory and she was confused and that's why she was pointing the finger at me. But now it was clear, Justina was malicious and she was willing to tell whatever lie necessary to bring me down.

The only way I was able to sit through the rest of Justina's testimony without flipping was to completely tune her out. I pretended to be somewhere else other than a courtroom at my trial.

This bitter hoe was gambling with my freedom and quite frankly she was winning. *Is this my destiny to spend the rest of my life behind bars? My freedom gone and left with no hope*, I thought as I put my head down wondering what would become of Aaliyah Mills Carter.

Precious

"This is some bullshit," I said to Supreme as we were leaving the courthouse. When we got outside we came up on Justina, Amir and her parents. My mind told me to keep walking but my mouth didn't listen.

"This is the type of daughter the two of you raised? One that would lie and let an innocent girl spend the rest of her life in jail over a boy?" I spit, eyeing Amir.

"How dare you. You want to blame us because you raised a murderer. I think she takes after her parents, all three of you," Chantal said, with a smug look on her face. I jumped at her ready to knock it right off.

"Precious, don't do it," Supreme belted holding me back.

"Yeah, I advise you to control your wife."

"What the fuck you say to me?" Supreme stepped in front of me and got in T-Roc's face.

"You heard what I said, you need to check your wife."

"My wife is good but if you don't get your people under control you gon' have to check yo' entire family if you know what I mean."

"Nigga, is you threatening my people?"

Supreme paused for a moment, nodded his head and responded calmly with a, "Yes." Then all you saw were fist swinging. It happened so fast that I couldn't even tell who threw the first punch.

"Stop!" Amir yelled out but that wasn't stopping nothing. It wasn't until Nico, Genesis and Lorenzo came running up that they were able to pull the two men apart.

"Motherfucker, don't you ever threaten my family!" T-Roc roared, while trying to straighten up his suit.

"Nigga, that wasn't a threat. You and yo' people keep fuckin wit' what's mine, it's a done deal. No threats…promises, nigga." Supreme made clear.

"Are you okay?" Lorenzo came over and asked me in the midst of all the chaos.

"I'm fine. I just don't know how much longer I can take my daughter being locked up."

"Your daughter is where she belongs," Chantal said walking up on us.

"Chantal, that's enough. You need to go."

"Lorenzo, why are you defending her? Her daughter killed a man and tried to murder Justina. Precious doesn't deserve sympathy."

"Why don't you go over there and be with your husband because we're having a private conversation that you're interrupting."

"Why don't you take your own advice and go be with your husband." I glanced over in Supreme's direction quickly and saw he was still in a deep conversation with Genesis.

"Lorenzo, I'ma go but I'll talk to you later."

"Call me if you need me."

"I will…thanks." As I walked away I could hear Chantal still running off at the mouth to Lorenzo and I didn't even know the two of them knew each other. But knowing Chantal they didn't she just wanted everybody to be #teamjustina and against Aaliyah. She was probably over there trying to convince Lorenzo of just that.

"Precious, hold up a minute," I heard Nico say before I reached Supreme.

"What's up?"

"That girl we were looking for has finally resurfaced."

"Are you serious?" my eyes widened in anticipation, wanting to believe all hope wasn't lost.

"Yes. I just had a chance to check my voicemail and my investigator left me a message. He knows exactly where she is and I'm going to get her."

"I'm coming with you."

"I don't know. If you tell Supreme he's gonna want to come too and I think we need to keep the number count low."

"I'll handle Supreme. Just wait for me. Give me five minutes and we can go." It worked out perfectly that Supreme and I arrived in separate cars so all I would have to do was come up with an excuse as to why I wasn't going straight home.

"A'ight. I'll be in my car. Call me when you're ready."

I couldn't believe we finally found her again. While I was in the hospital Nico broke the news to me that the one person who could get Aaliyah out of jail had fell off the radar. It was like she vanished and nobody could find her anywhere. That shit had me depressed for the last few weeks. At the time I was relieved I didn't tell Supreme about the possible lead because when it fell through I knew he would've found a way to blame me. Now that Nico was able to locate her again I wasn't letting anything fuck it up.

"Hey, not to interrupt but I wanted to check on my husband."

"We were just finishing up. I know this is tough for both of you but hang in there. Trust me you have all of our support."

"I appreciate that, Genesis. I know this must be hard for you especially since T-Roc is a friend of yours."

"I've known Aaliyah since she was a little girl and yes she is her mother's daughter but I also know she is not a killer. I put that on my own life."

"Thank you for saying that."

"It's the truth. I don't know what happened that night in the hotel room but what I do know Aaliyah didn't pull the trigger. We'll get to the truth. I just pray it will be in enough time to save Aaliyah," Genesis said, before rubbing my shoulder and walking away.

"Are you okay?"

"I'll be fine once our daughter is out of jail. Until then no I'm not okay."

"I feel the same way but we'll get through this and our daughter will come home."

"I hear you," he huffed. "Listen, I have a few things to take care of. I'll see you at home later on."
Wow that was much easier than I expected. I didn't even have to

bother trying to come up with an excuse because Supreme was off doing his own thing anyway I thought as I headed towards my car.

When I reached my car the first thing I did was call Nico. A few minutes later he pulled his car up and I followed behind him anxious to get to the final destination. When we got on the Brooklyn Bridge I realized the girl was no longer staying in the City and wondered if she was hiding out. We eventually got on Flatbush Avenue until we reached Park Slope. We turned down a quiet tree lined street that seemed more appropriate for a suburban family trying to escape the big city instead of a girl who facilitated in helping someone commit murder.

I noticed Nico motioning me to park my car and I did so a few feet away from where he had found a parking space. Before getting out I reached for the 9mm I kept in a secret compartment for emergency purposes. Hopefully I wouldn't need it but being prepared was always a must.

"Are you ready?" Nico asked as I stepped out the car.

"I'm good."

"Glad to hear. But listen just to give you a heads up I got three of my men with me."

"I can understand now why you didn't want Supreme here."

"Yeah, it would've been too much because I brought these men just in case we have to do some damage. I know for a fact the girl is in that apartment," he said pointing to a spot three buildings down. "We're getting to her by any means necessary so it might get ugly."

"I have no problem with that but remember we need her alive."

"True, but she doesn't need to know that. Now you ready."

"Following you." When we got to the front door, Nico's goons were already there with the front entrance open. I didn't even ask how they got in. All I did was watch. Nico and I had been on these sorts of missions more than once but this time the stakes were much higher. We all got on the elevator and one of the guys pushed the seventh floor. Nico and I stood in the front while the three men were behind us with their arms to the side and fist clutched. Their muscles were bulging through their black ribbed shirts and their faces showed no emotions.

When the elevator doors opened Nico stepped to the side letting the goons know to lead the way.

When we got to the apartment at the very end of the hall I was expecting one of them to knock on the door instead that two hundred and fifty pound nigga of pure muscles kicked that motherfucker open.

"Get the fuck down and put your hands on top of your head!" One of the goons barked, as all three men pulled out their guns simultaneously. They all had a gun in each hand. I noticed two women that looked to be in their early twenties and both screamed out in fear as the weapons were pointed at them. They were sitting on the couch with the television on and seemed to be eating. But they both dropped their plates and the open cans of soda spilled on the hardwood floors from the shock.

"Please don't kill us," one of the girls pleaded as they both jumped to the floor as they were directed to do.

"Danny, close the door and keep watch out front," Nico ordered one of the goons. The other one did a search of the apartment while the other kept his guns aimed at the women.

"Its all clear," the goon said after looking around the apartment.

"Which one of you is Jessica Vasquez?" Nico

asked, bending down looking both women in their eyes.

"She is," one of the girls said quickly.

"Is that true? Are you Jessica Vasquez?" Nico's authoritative voice seemed to make the girl resistant to answer. But when that gun touched her temple she admitted the truth and then the tears began flowing.

"Please don't kill me. I haven't done anything wrong."

"Can I please leave? I don't have anything to do with this," the other girl begged.

"Neither one of you are going anywhere until you tell me what I want to know. So we're clear, if either of you lie, these men will kill you. Then we will find out who your family is and kill them too." Nico warned without hesitation.

"Jessica, tell them whatever they want to know. I don't want to die!"

"What do you want to know?" Jessica sniffled.

"Who paid you off for helping them kill Sway Stone?"

"You helped somebody kill Sway Stone!" Jessica's friend shrieked. Jessica's eyes became enlarged as if in disbelief that we were here about Sway.

"I don't know what you're talking about," Jessica finally said, sounding totally unconvincing.

"This is my only warning to you and then I'm going to let these men start blasting…"

"Oh gosh, please don't kill me," Jessica's friend bawled interrupting Nico's threat. "I have nothing to do with this. Jessica answer his question. I don't want to die!"

"Like I was saying. This is your only warning. Tell the truth or my man here is going to put a bullet right there," Nico said, tapping Jessica's forehead. So the girl knew Nico wasn't playing the goon took the tip of his gun and massaged the center of her forehead with it.

"Okay, I'll tell you what I know but you have to promise you won't kill us."

"I'm not promising anything until you tell me what I want to know. This is not a negotiation."

"Would you please tell him what he wants to know!" Jessica's friend cried out.

"I didn't know Sway Stone was going to die…I swear. All I was told was that I could make some quick money if I gave them the hotel room key. It wasn't until after the shootings did I realize what I had done. By then it was too late. Then the money just kept coming in to keep me quiet. I knew I should've left New York for good," Jessica said, shaking her head.

"I need a name. Who gave you the money?" Nico was growing impatient and so was I.

"Tell them!" Jessica's friend chimed in as we all waited, eager to hear the name. And when Jessica finally said it, my mouth dropped. It made no sense to me. I was more confused than ever.

Aaliyah

"Will I be taking the stand tomorrow?" I asked my attorney as we went over the witness list for the defense, which didn't consist of much. Mr. Anderson's argument was always that the prosecution's case would be weak but after a week of testimony their case seemed pretty strong to me. The police officers testified that I was holding the murder weapon when they entered the hotel room. DNA was found under my nails from when I scratched Justina's neck and lets not forget I was identified as the shooter from the actual victim. From where I was sitting the case seemed pretty airtight.

"Aaliyah, I'm not sure if I want you to take the stand."

"Why not? You've been prepping me for the last couple weeks. I basically have my testimony memorized. I need to defend myself especially with all the lies that have been said about me."

"I understand your frustration but I'm afraid that on cross examination your temper might get the best of you. Trust me, the prosecutor is going to come at you hard. She will throw everything at you to shake you up."

"True, but what is it looking like for me right now and tell me the truth?"

"In terms of a verdict?"

"Yes, do you think the juror will find me guilty?"

"Honestly it could go either way. Justina didn't come across as completely credible. The prosecution wasn't able to explain why there wasn't traces of gun powder residue found on your hands or clothes…that's significant."

"Is it significant enough to get a not guilty verdict?"

"When I first took this case I told you I would never lie to you. When it comes to jurors you never know. Justina testifying that it was you who shot her is extremely damaging unless the jurors believe her testimony to be a lie. Although I didn't find her credible I can't say if they did or they didn't. You might also end up with a hung jury."

"I don't want a hung jury because the prosecutor will only retry the case and I'll be stuck behind bars waiting all over again. I need a not guilty. So I want to testify, Mr. Anderson."

"Are you sure? I tell all my clients when you take the stand it's a huge risk. It can work in your favor or end up costing you your freedom. But whatever decision you make, Aaliyah I'll support it. Get some rest tonight. We have a big day tomorrow. We begin presenting our case so think about what you want to do. If you do want to take the stand, you'll be the first witness tomorrow morning."

"I'll make sure I'm ready. Oh, and Mr. Anderson, have you heard any news about my grandfather?"

"He's still in a coma. I know it's difficult but don't think about that right now. Your grandfather would want you to focus on this case."

"I know. I just wish he could be here with me."

"He is in spirit…remember that. Now I'll see you in the morning."

When I got back to my cell my body was tired but my mind wouldn't let me sleep. Soon I would know my fate and to me it seemed doomed. I had already spent one birthday behind bars and the idea of spending sixty or seventy more almost made me want to slit my wrist. The thought of Justina living a carefree life with Amir while I rotted away in prison made me want to vomit. I felt betrayed by both of them, Justina for straight up lying on me, and Amir for turning his back on me to support Justina. It made me wonder if anybody truly believed I was innocent besides my grandfather who never swayed in his belief that I was set up. My eyes began to get heavy as I thought about the what ifs and eventually I fell into a deep sleep.

"I want to testify," were the first words out of my mouth to my attorney when I sat down. Mr. Anderson simply smiled at me and then turned to the judge.

"Your Honor, the first witness we will be calling is Chantal Morgan."

"Your Honor, Mrs. Morgan isn't anywhere on the defense witness list."

"Your Honor, can I approach the bench?'

"Please do, Mr. Anderson," and the judge motioned for the prosecutor to do the same. I was perplexed as to why my lawyer was calling Chantal as a witness but she was Justina's mother and he might wanted to use her to catch Justina in some lies. I looked back and saw Justina and her mother exchanging words as we waited to hear the judge's ruling. Part of me was hoping the judge would delay letting Chantal testify because I was ready to take the stand and defend myself. I thought once the jurors heard my side of the story they would believe me and know I was not the person that pulled the trigger.

"Chantal Morgan, please take the stand," we heard the judge announce and I let out a disappointing sigh. I wanted to speak with my attorney about what was going on but it was as if he was purposely not making any eye contact with me. He didn't come back to the table. He stood in the center of the courtroom until Chantal was sworn in and sat down. Chantal seemed to be at ease and not concerned in the least as to why she was called to testify. Mr. Anderson began with very lightweight questions like her relation to Justina, her marital status, shit that made me want to yawn. I had no idea where he was going with this and I felt like it was wasting time and annoying the jurors who were probably ready for this trial to be over so they could get back to their normal lives.

"Mrs. Morgan, who were you seeing twice a week at the Mandarin Oriental Hotel from November 2010 to May of 2011."

"Excuse me?"

"Maybe these hotel receipts from the American Express card in your husband's name will refresh your memory," Mr. Anderson stated, handing them to Chantal. "Those are your signatures on the receipts… correct?" What started off as lightweight questioning had quickly turned heavyweight. Chantal's cool, calm and confident demeanor appeared to be slowly falling apart.

"Mrs. Morgan, answer the question," the judge said looking over at Chantal.

"I was meeting the man I was having an affair with."

"I see. You are married to T-Roc, Justina's father, is that correct?"

"Yes I am." I glanced back and even from a distance I could see flames burning in T-Roc's eyes.

"So you were meeting your lover at the same hotel Mr. Stone was killed and your daughter was shot."

"Yes, it's an ironic coincidence."

"There is no such thing as a coincidence in a murder trial, Mrs. Morgan. Isn't it true that at the Mandarin Oriental Hotel is where you first met Jessica Vasquez?"

"Who is that?" Chantal asked casually as if she had never heard the name before.

"Ms. Vasquez worked at the front desk of the hotel during that time and several months after."

"I might've spoken to her in passing when I was coming in or leaving the hotel."

"That was the only time?"

"Yes."

"So your testimony is you had no further conversations with Ms. Vasquez besides…"

"Yes, that is my testimony," Chantal answered before Mr. Anderson finished his question. Right after Chantal said that the courtroom door opened and Nico walked in with a Hispanic looking woman. They sat down in the back. I looked back at Chantal and she had the look of death on her face.

"Isn't it true you gave Ms. Vaquez $10,000 in cash and for the last several months you've been depositing $6,000 a month in her bank account? Before you answer the question, Mrs. Morgan why don't you take a look at these banking records and how the deposits made to Ms. Vasquez's account match up with the cash withdrawals you made from your account."

"Ms. Vasquez somehow found out who I was married to and began blackmailing me. She threatened to tell my husband or go to the press about my affair so I paid her off. It's unfortunate for my family that it has to come out here in open court." Chantal's testimony was getting so juicy to me that I almost forgot that I was the one on trial. But I still didn't understand how Chantal's scandalous affair had anything to do with Sway's murder until Mr. Anderson gradually put the pieces together.

"So the money Ms. Vasquez received from you was to keep quiet about your affair?"

"Yes."

"I see where your daughter learned to lie so well," Mr. Anderson commented taking a jab at Chantal.

"Objection, Your honor, badgering the witness."

"Sustained!"

"Isn't it true, Mrs. Morgan, that you gave Ms. Vasquez $10,000 to give you the room key to the penthouse suite Mr. Stone was staying in the night he was murdered?" you could hear loud gasps circulating the courtroom after Mr. Anderson hit Chantal with that question. "Isn't it also true that you continued to pay her $6,000 a month after the murder so Ms. Vasquez wouldn't go to the police and tell them that it was you; who murdered Sway Stone and shot your own daughter?" Between Mr.

Anderson's questions all I heard was objections from the prosecutor, Justina crying out for my attorney to leave her mother alone and the judge basically telling everybody to shut the fuck up but the ruckus continued until we were all silenced by Chantal's words.

"It was all an accident. I would never hurt Justina. It was Precious and her spoiled brat of a daughter Aaliyah that were supposed to pay. Precious took the man that I loved away from me and Aaliyah was trying to do the same to Justina and I couldn't allow that to happen."

"Your Honor, if possible can we have a break at this time?" the prosecutor requested right when Chantal's testimony was getting good.

"Don't interrupt me…I would like to continue," Chantal stated in an eerie way. A craze glaze seemed to come over her as if she wasn't quite herself.

"Your Honor, I believe the court would like to hear what Mrs. Morgan has to say," my attorney said what all of us were thinking.

"I agree. Mrs. Morgan, continue."

"It all started when I met Lorenzo and we fell in love." I couldn't believe what I was hearing. Chantal was seeing Lorenzo too. I shook my head praying that what I thought was about to happen wouldn't. I listened as Chantal continued. "We began seeing each other. We would meet twice a week sometimes more at the Mandarin. It was there I began talking to Jessica. At first it was casual but then it became much more frequent."

"At what point did you ask Ms. Vasquez to give you a key to Sway Stone's hotel room?" Mr. Anderson asked wanting to skip over the long version and get right to the point but Chantal wasn't having it.

"If you want the truth then let me tell my story. This is so much bigger than Sway Stone." Chantal's defiant tone and shameless facial expression made her appear as if she was going over the edge. It made me reflect back to the story I had read a few years ago. She had tried to run over her ex fiancée with her car after he left her at the altar for that movie star Tyler Blake. For whatever reason she got off but clearly the crazy was still there.

"By all means continue," Mr. Anderson said realizing it was counterproductive to try and reason with an irrational person.

"As I was saying I began somewhat of an unintentional friendship with Jessica because I was frequenting the hotel often. Then Lorenzo broke off our relationship and I found out he had been seeing Precious Mills." My head dropped, as the one thing I was praying wouldn't be revealed, had been.

"What in the hell is she talking about?" I heard my dad ask my mom. Even in a calm tone his anger made his voice loud.

"Supreme, this isn't the time," I heard my mother reply. Although I hated the fact she had an affair with Lorenzo I never wanted her to get busted like this.

"Everybody quiet," the judge ordered banging his gavel. "If you can't be quiet I will have you escorted out of my courtroom. Now continue Mrs. Morgan."

"Lorenzo didn't even tell me why he broke things off between us. It wasn't until Jessica called me because Lorenzo came to the hotel with another woman and she thought I should know. I told her if they came in again to take a picture of the woman because I wanted to know who she was. I was stunned to find out it was Precious. I thought she was supposed to be happily married to Supreme. Then she shared a daughter with Nico who was in business with Lorenzo but I guess that didn't matter. Like mother like daughter, if they see something they want they take it no matter who it might hurt. And when Justina called me hysterical about catching Aaliyah trying to seduce Amir I knew it was time to teach mother and daughter a lesson and at the same time win back Lorenzo," Chantal smiled with that loco look plastered on her face.

"See during those months I was seeing Lorenzo he told me how much he despised Sway Stone because he was responsible for the death of Dior, the only woman he ever loved, that was until he met me. He said no matter what he had to do Sway would pay for Dior's death. I thought it would be my gift to Lorenzo to kill Sway and a gift to myself to take away what Precious loved the most...her daughter."

"So how did your daughter Justina end up shot?" Mr. Anderson asked. I guess he wasn't interested in hearing Chantal's soap opera story although everybody else in the courtroom seemed to be.

"Don't rush me. I haven't gotten to that part yet," Chantal snapped, tossing her hair to the side. She then sat up extra straight and began fidgeting with the big ass diamond ring sitting on her wedding finger. I didn't know what was going on with Chantal but the screws were definitely loose and we could all see it with our very own eyes. The woman was in the middle of having a nervous breakdown.

I could hear whimpering coming from behind me and I turned around and saw Justina with her head down leaning on her father's shoulder. If I didn't hate her so much I would've felt sorry for Justina.

"I'm not trying to rush you, Mrs. Morgan."

"Then stop interrupting me. That entire night is still a little blurry for me. Jessica had informed me weeks prior that Sway Stone would be having a party at the hotel but it wasn't until that day did I decide he would die and so would Aaliyah. Once I made up my mind I popped several pills, you know to calm my nerves. I already had the gun. All I needed was for Jessica to call me once Aaliyah arrived at the hotel."

"Did Ms. Vasquez know you were coming to the hotel to murder Sway Stone and Aaliyah?"

"Of course not, nobody knew but me and honestly I wasn't sure if I would be able to go through with it."

"But you did go through with it?"

"It didn't exactly work out. I mean Aaliyah is still alive," Chantal said in a sinister voice as she eyed me. "But..." There was a long pause and Chantal started rubbing her hands together and then she exhaled.

"But what, Mrs. Morgan?" Mr. Anderson questioned after an extended period of silence.

"I have nothing further to say. I'm exercising my 5th Amendment right against self-incrimination. So we're done here." Just like that out of the blue Chantal shut it down.

"I have no further questions for this witness," Mr. Anderson said, walking back to the table.

"I have no questions for this witness," the prosecutor added sounding as if all the life had been sucked out of her.

"Your Honor, based on the testimony of Mrs. Morgan I ask that all the charges be dismissed against my client."

"Court is adjourned until two o'clock. I would like to see you both in my chambers...now," the judge ordered.

"I'll come speak with you as soon as I know something," Mr. Anderson said before the officers escorted me out. I looked around and thought that there was a very good chance I could walk out of jail a free woman today but at what cost. The chaos had already ensued. My mother was chasing after my father but it seemed all he wanted to do was get out of the courtroom. Genesis was standing between Lorenzo and Nico who appeared to be ready for a twelve round boxing match. But the most bizarre part was as I turned the corner to leave I caught a glimpse of Chantal who had a menacing smile on her face. That bitch was truly crazy or she was the devil. Either way the damage was done and I knew this was just the beginning of the worse kind of nightmare erupting.

Precious

"Supreme wait…I can explain," I said, grabbing his arm as he was trying to leave out the courtroom.

"Is what Chantal said true?" I waited for a few moments because I didn't know how to answer Supreme's question. I was fighting whether to tell the truth or lie. "Answer the question," he insisted. It didn't help that Supreme was being so calm yet direct.

"Yes, but we were having so many problems. I was only…."

"Save it," Supreme said cutting me off. "I don't need an explanation…you're dead to me."

"You don't mean that." The expression on Supreme's face, after all the bullshit we'd been through he had never looked at me this way before. It was if he was looking through me like I no longer existed. "Supreme, please say something. We have to talk about this." But my words seemed to have fallen on deaf ears because he said nothing else to me and instead walked out the courtroom doors.

I stood there frozen. For so many months I felt my marriage was over that Supreme and I were done but it wasn't until this very moment that it hit me, I was still very much in love with my husband and to be without him was a reality I couldn't face. My determination gave me the strength to move swiftly and go after Supreme. My once frozen body was now in motion as I headed in his direction.

"Not so fast." My body jerked back from a strong force pulling at my shoulder.

"Nico, you need to calm down!" He pulled me so hard for a second it felt as if my shoulder had been dislocated.

"I need to calm down…no, Precious, you need to calm it the fuck down. What the hell were you thinking carrying on with Lorenzo!"

"Nico, we share a child together not a bed. The only person I owe an explanation to is my husband…the man you're keeping me from right now. So excuse me I need to get to Supreme."

"That man doesn't want you. Supreme is done with you and I don't blame him." When what Nico said registered with me I thought I was about to choke to death. It felt as if somebody repeatedly kicked me in the stomach while punching me in the chest.

"How can you say something so cruel?"

"How? very easily. You've been fucking a man I do business with."

"This isn't about you. I didn't set out to have sex with Lorenzo because I knew you all did business together…it just happened."

"You're a grown woman and you still haven't learned any self-control. And you wonder why Aaliyah is in the fucked up predicament she is now. You're her role model."

"So now what happened to Aaliyah is my fault? What about that crazy bitch Chantal and her daughter who both clearly set Aaliyah up…what about them? None of this is their fault? You're so pissed at me for sleeping with Lorenzo that you're hitting way below the belt. But I'm not dealing with this shit from you right now."

I hurried off not waiting to give Nico the last word. It didn't matter because he said enough. *That man doesn't want you. Supreme is done with you and I don't blame him*. Those words kept replaying in my head. For a moment I thought I was going to run in a corner and vomit. I had to get some fresh air and headed outside to catch my breath.

"My poor sister, things aren't going well for you today, are they." As I stood on top of the stairs holding on to the rail my first thought was to kick Maya down them when she walked up on me talking that bullshit.

"Maya, this is not the time."

"I know. Under the circumstances I'm sure you don't want to talk to anybody. I mean Chantal called you out for the whore you are in open court. Supreme is finally done with you and Nico sees exactly what type of baby mama he has. On the bright side as least Aaliyah will be getting out of jail. But what is the poor girl coming home to, certainly not a mother and a father. That home is irretrievably broken. And poor Xavier, his daddy will end up marrying another woman, starting a family with her and forget all about his first-born son. You have truly fucked up now, Precious."

"If we weren't standing in front of a courthouse surrounded by police officers I would kill you right now. But that's the beautiful thing about life; God willing there is always another day. So lucky for you Maya, you have one more day to live. But start counting the days down because the clock is ticking."

"Is that my clock you hear ticking or is it

yours," Maya laughed before walking off. As much as I despised Maya I was glad she approached me because I needed a reminder as to why I couldn't pity myself and get weak. I constantly had to watch my back, which meant there was no time for slipping. As I thought about what my next move would be I saw Genesis walking in my direction.

"Fuck, I'm not in the mood for another round of this bullshit," I moaned. If Genesis wasn't already staring directly in my eyes I would've tried to find a way to get ghost but I had no other choice but to deal with yet another confrontation.

"How are you?" I was expecting Geneis's voice to have an attack tone to it but it didn't. It actually sounded full of concern, which I welcomed.

"I've been better."

"I'm sure. Listen, we have a couple hours before court resumes. How about we go have some lunch."

"That sounds good."

"Let's go, I'll drive."

When Genesis and I got to the restaurant we sat at a table in the back. I was relieved it was practically empty. The tranquil environment put me at ease and at the moment that's what I needed. "Thank you for bringing me here."

"Thanks for coming. I could tell by the look in your eyes when you first saw me, you weren't interested in having a conversation."

"It wasn't that. I thought you were going to rip into me like Supreme and Nico. I didn't feel like dealing with that."

"I have no right to judge you, Precious. Every day I make choices that most people wouldn't agree with. But it's what I choose to do and I'm willing to accept whatever consequences come with it. Although you have that same right, I don't believe you thought about the consequences before you acted." I glanced out the window while taking a sip of my wine pondering what Genesis said.

"You're right," I admitted. "I'm not proud of what I've done but this isn't all on me. Our marriage has been shaky for some time now. Supreme seemed to have checked out a long time ago. I really believed our marriage was over but I wasn't ready to give up. Especially when everything happened with Aaliyah, I wanted to fight for my family. I do love Supreme but the thing is I love Lorenzo too."

"I was hoping you wouldn't say that."

"Why?"

"Because that makes everything much more complicated."

"I thought once we got Aaliyah exonerated we could be a family again and get our lives back to normal. Who knew clearing her name would destroy any chance of that," I said, shaking my head. "All because of Chantal's crazy ass. It's wasn't enough she set my daughter up but she needed to take me down with her."

"I was certain that Aaliyah didn't kill anybody but never in a million years did I think Chantal was the real killer."

"And all because of her sick obsession with Lorenzo. Did you know they were seeing each other?"

"No I didn't. But Lorenzo is very private when it comes to his personal life. I believe the only reason he spoke to me about you was because the relationship got serious and he had his reservations because of the Nico factor."

"Nico," I sighed, reflecting on the harsh words we exchanged. "Nico seems to believe that he deserves an explanation. Supreme is my husband and Nico is the father of my oldest child. Yes, because of our history I'll always have love for Nico and respect him for being Aaliyah's dad but he tried to crucify me today."

"I've known Nico for a very long time now.

We're not only business partners but also he's one of my closest friends and I believe he always thought you all would get back together someday. It's easier for him to accept you're married to Supreme and a certain loyalty comes with that but to find out about Lorenzo, it crushed him. I knew it would and that's why I never told him about it."

"That had to be difficult for you. I mean I know you're close to both of them."

"It is. Lorenzo is a good man. Like myself, he's been dealt a lot of tough blows in life but he soldiers through them. To be honest with you, Precious, I was hoping it would be nothing more than a fling between the two of you and both of you would move on, that way nobody would get hurt. But this is a nightmare come true. No matter what happens between you and Lorenzo the damage is done."

"I know," I admitted putting my head down. "The only thing that makes it worth it is that my baby is coming home. If it took Chantal airing out my dirty deeds to set Aaliyah free then so be it."

"True indeed. I hate what happened to Aaliyah. You're going to have to be patient with her, Precious. After spending all those months in jail I hope you realize that she'll never be the same again."

"What do you mean?"

"I spent the majority of my teenage years locked up in a juvenile facility and it stole my innocence. Aaliyah has been in prison for months for a crime she didn't commit surrounded by real criminals. That would harden anybody."

"You're so right and every time I think about that all this anger that's built up inside of me just wants to explode. All I want to know is at what point did Chantal and Justina begin conspiring together. I believe they both belong in jail."

"And they could both very well end up there although I'm sure T-Roc will do everything in his power to make sure that doesn't happen."

"After that show Chantal put on in the courtroom T-Roc should handcuff her himself and personally deliver her to the women's prison facility."

"T-Roc and I go way back and I know how he moves. Trust me, he's already been on the phone with the best criminal attorney in the state of New York who's advising him on what to do next."

"Chantal admitted to shooting Sway Stone and her own daughter because in her sick mind she wanted to prove her love for Lorenzo and punish me. Why would T-Roc waste a dime trying to get her off?"

"In a nutshell…ego. Chantal has embarrassed him enough. T-Roc is not going to allow it to continue."

"If T-Roc knows what is good for him, he'll make sure Chantal goes to jail and stays there. Because if he gets that nutcase off I'm putting her on the same list Maya is on."

"I feel you. If it were my child, heads would roll. Nobody would be immune but I don't recommend you follow that path. Let the legal system do what it does first. If for some reason they fuck it up then we can go back to your list. But for now you have to fall back."

"I don't know if I'll be able to do that. The system already failed Aaliyah and the only reason the truth came out is because Quentin found the missing link to bring all this shit together. So let's just say I'm not really confident with their services."

"Under the circumstances, that's a fair statement but, Precious, you have way too much to lose. Trust me on this. Let the legal system do their job. You go out here playing vigilante you're going to end up in the exact same place you fought to get Aaliyah out of."

"Point taken. I'll give it some time to see what happens but Chantal and Justina will pay for what they did to Aaliyah, so for their sakes they better pray that punishment comes from the court of law, because my penance is a life for a life."

"I got that. All I'm trying to do is make sure Aaliyah and Xavier both grow up with their mommy."

"I feel you but let's go," I said, looking down at my watch. "Court is about to resume and you know I can't be late."

"And I don't want you to, so let's go."

When we got back to the courtroom the first thing I did was look for Supreme. My eyes were darting all around but there wasn't a trace of Supreme. *There is no way he would miss this. Supreme knows that Aaliyah needs his support and so do I.* I went to take my seat with a heavy heart. I felt a pair of eyes burning a hole through me and when I turned to see who it was, I realized it was Nico. Before I turned my head back around I checked out the other side of the courtroom and noticed T-Roc. Chantal and Justina were nowhere to be found which stunned me. I thought about what Genesis's said and he might've been right. Had T-Roc been in touch with an attorney and started building a defense for his wife and daughter. If he had he was a piece of work.

"All rise…" I heard the officer say as my mind

was still struggling to figure out where Chantal and Justina had disappeared to. Before I gave my full attention to the judge I scanned the courtroom one last time and Lorenzo wasn't in attendance either. Genesis and Amir were standing together and right before I turned away I noticed Supreme walk through the doors. *Praise The Lord Supreme is here, Aaliayh would've been devastated*, I thought before sitting down.

"Damn, I hope this shit is finally over and Aaliyah will be able to come home," I whispered under my breath before saying a quiet prayer. I was also praying that Supreme would come sit next to me but when I glanced towards the door again he was sitting down in the back.

"After speaking with both attorneys in my chambers and due to the testimony of Chantal Morgan I move to have all charges against Aaliyah Mills Carter dismissed with prejudice. Court dismissed," he said pounding down his gavel.

"My baby is finally coming home," I said out loud with the biggest smile on my face. I wanted everybody to hear the joy in my voice. At this moment I wanted to celebrate Aaliyah but soon my focus would be on making sure everybody responsible for having her spend all those months behind bars paid in full.

Aaliyah

"*I* can't believe I'm going home," I hugged Mr. Anderson and said.

"You deserve it. "

"So I can just go?"

"We have some paperwork to fill out but yes you will be going home today. Now go hug your family. I know you want to," Mr. Anderson smiled.

I found myself walking slowly towards my family. For whatever reason I felt nervous. It was weird. Spending all those months in jail made a small part of me feel like I didn't know them anymore.

"I'm so happy you're coming home," my mom said, greeting me with a big hug and kiss. "We missed you so much. Xavier is going to be so happy to see his big sister," she gushed.

"My baby girl is coming home where she belongs." Nico squeezed me so tight, I felt like I couldn't breathe. "My world has not been the same without you in it."

"Neither has mine," Amir said, coming forward. "Aaliyah, I'm thrilled you're coming home but I knew you would."

"Don't speak to me." I snapped. I heard the sound of aahs coming from all around me. "You walked away from me when I was at my lowest point in jail because you wanted to stand by your sweet and innocent Justina. While I sat at the table with my attorney fighting for my freedom you stood and held hands with my enemy, the snake responsible for putting me in this predicament. Now that I'm free you have the nerves to show me love. Take that bullshit someplace else."

"Aaliyah! Don't speak to Amir like that," my mother said, taken aback by the words that just came out of my mouth.

"It's okay, Mrs. Mills, I understand why she's upset. Aaliyah, I just hope one day you can forgive me."

"It ain't gon' never happen so stop hoping. Now excuse me I want to go speak with my dad." I hurried off to the back of the courtroom and ran into the arms of my father. I needed his love just as much as I knew he needed mine.

"Are you okay?" he whispered in my ear as I

held him tightly.

"No, but I'm going to get there."

He held me by my arms and pulled away from my embrace before saying, "I'm sorry."

"Why are you apologizing?"

"I know lately I haven't been here for you the way I should and I'm sorry. But I love you more than you could ever know."

"I know you do and, daddy, please don't leave us. I know what you found out in court has hurt you so bad but please, I'm begging you not to leave us."

"I will never leave you or Xavier. The two of you give me a reason to live, never doubt that." Then my father held me and I knew that meant he was gone, he wasn't coming back home and once again my heart was broken.

3 Months Later

As I sat outside watching Xavier doing flips into the infinity pool I smiled at how happy he seemed under the circumstances. He was a soldier just like our father. Him being gone seemed to hit me the hardest. I was still expecting my dad to come back home but he wasn't. He did spend a lot of time with us especially Xavier, they seemed closer than ever but it wasn't the same. Then there was my grandfather he had been in a coma for months. The only reason they wouldn't take him off of life support was because the doctor said that there was still brain activity. That made us optimistic but it didn't help when all you wanted him to do was wake up. Before the tears began to escape my eyes I heard my IPhone ringing. A number I didn't recognize came across the screen but I decided to answer.

"Hello."

"Is this Aaliyah?"

"Who's asking?" the voice sounded familiar but I didn't like the fact they were calling my phone but unsure if they were speaking to me.

"This is Peaches."

"Omigoodness! Peaches, how are you?"

"I'm good. When I heard you got out I wanted to call you but I couldn't find your number anywhere. But I just found it and so you know I had to call you. How you doing?"

"Things are cool. I'm free so that makes things great."

"So what have you been up to?"

"Nothing really, I'm still getting used to being out and not locked up. I'm debating on whether I'm going to start school this fall or try modeling again. I haven't figured anything out yet. How about you?"

"I have a lot going on and I want you to be a part of it. You up for lunch?"

"No I'm here with my lil' brother. I can do dinner."

"That works for me. I'll hit you in a couple hours and we can decide where to go."

"Cool, I'll talk to you later." When I hung up with Peaches I got excited about hanging out with her tonight. Since Justina and Amir were no longer my best friends the only people I had been around the last few months were family. It would be nice to be around somebody my own age.

"Xavier, be careful," I heard my mother call out, interrupting my thoughts. "I always get scared seeing him do those flips in the pool. I'm afraid he's going to hurt himself," my mother said sitting down next to me.

"I wasn't expecting you back for another couple of hours."

"The meeting at my attorney's office wrapped

up sooner than I thought it would."

"What were you meeting with your attorney about?"

"Your father has filed for legal separation. It's that step we have to take before getting a divorce."

"I can't believe you guys are really going through with this," I said, shaking my head.

"I can't force your father to stay with me. He's made a decision and as much as I don't agree with it, there isn't anything I can do."

"Too bad you didn't think about that before you cheated."

"Aaliyah, your father and I were having problems way before that and not to excuse it but that's one of the reasons why I cheated. When you're not being fulfilled at home you tend to go elsewhere. You're too young to understand any of this but one day when you get married you will."

"I don't ever want to get married. Not if it's going to end up the way it did for you and dad."

"You say that now but when you meet that special man that captures your heart all reasoning goes out the door."

"I don't want to be hurt by a man again."

"Are you talking about Amir?" I looked away not answering my mother's question. "Amir didn't mean to hurt you. He's young and he's going to make mistakes. You've known him almost all your life. Don't throw that friendship away because of his poor judgment in one situation."

"So am I supposed to forgive Justina too?" I asked sarcastically.

"Of course not, that's totally different."

"How is it different? Amir stopped coming to see me in jail because of Justina. He chose her over me. How can I forgive that?"

"Aaliyah, it's not a competition. You have to understand the dilemma Amir was in. You're his best friend and Justina was his girlfriend. He cared about both of you. He had no idea that Justina was setting you up."

"Yeah, she and her mother set me up and they're both still walking around free while I had to sit in jail for months when I did nothing wrong. What sense does any of that make? I told Amir I was innocent."

"And he knew that but I don't think he believed Justina was straight up lying. He wanted to give her the benefit of the doubt but he realizes he was wrong."

"I wonder now that the truth is out has he turned his back on Justina like he did me."

"The only way you're going to find out what's going on with Amir is if you sit down and talk to him."

"I'm not ready to do that and I don't know when I will be."

"I understand but don't become bitter and close yourself off because of what happened. You're so young and smart. You can accomplish whatever your heart desires and you'll have our complete support."

"I don't know what I want to do."

"There's no rush. Take your time."

"I'll figure something out."

"I know you will." My mother gave me a warm smile. I knew she meant well but I had this bottled up animosity towards her, Amir and just about everybody else. Part of me was mad at the world and the fact that Chantal wasn't in jail didn't help. "I was thinking the three of us could go out to dinner tonight," my mother suggested, as if she could tell my mind was wandering off to another place.

"I would but Peaches an old friend of mine called and invited me to go out."

"Peaches...I've never heard you mention her before."

"She's somebody I knew from when I did some modeling," I lied. My mother would have a shit fit if I told her she was my old roomie from jail.

"I think that would be good for you. You haven't been out with any of your friends since you got out of jail. You need to try and get some normalcy back in your life."

"Well hopefully this girl date will be the start of that," I beamed. I meant that shit too. I wanted to feel young, sexy and full of life again. Moping around the house and doing everything with my mother and brother was cool at first but now it was becoming redundant. It was time for me to start living life again.

As I drove over the George Washington Bridge I was blasting Trouble's mixtape, 431 Days that I had downloaded online. Because I was sitting in the house all day everyday, I had become a hip-hop music connoisseur and his shit was by far my favorite. While Hustle & Ambition blared from my speakers, the words resonated with me because currently I had neither. It felt like I was lost in the world with no direction and that was a fucked up feeling. I had the song on repeat as I made my way into the City and headed towards Soho. I needed to get my mind right and escape this funk I was in. Jail took away eight months of my life; I didn't want it to take eight more.

When I pulled up to the restaurant I parked my car across the street in a parking garage. That was the main thing I hated about coming into the city you could never find parking and paying was hella high. But I wasn't going to take any chances on my new all white Range Rover getting towed. It was a gift from Nico. He called it my coming home present. When I stepped out the sunshine hit my face and a boost of energy came over me. That was one of the great things about summertime, at 7 pm the sun still shined bright. For the first time in a while I did actually feel cute today. I had on some skinny white jeans with a V-neck white tee and some bubblegum pink open toe platform heels to give my outfit some pop. I had my curls lifted high in a ponytail with a couple of loose curls falling over my eye. My hoop diamond stud earrings and soft pink lip-gloss complimented the look perfectly. My outer appearance was on point now all I had to do was get my inner spirit right.

When I entered the restaurant I noticed Peaches sitting at a corner yapping hard on the phone. Whoever she was talking to had her in deep conversation, so much so it took her a minute to even see that I was about to sit down. She held her finger up, signaling for me to give her a second. I sat my purse down and called the waitress over to order me a drink. As I was about to flip through the menu to decide what I would be ordering I damn near lost my appetite. I had to do a double take. *Why does bullshit seem to follow me? Is that really Amir and Justina sitting together having dinner, please let my eyes be playing tricks on me.* But they weren't. The shit was real and I was ready to turn this restaurant out.

"Hey girl! I'm used to seeing you in orange jumpsuits but you walked in here looking like a star," Peaches smiled standing up to give me a hug. It took me a sec to stand up too because I was too busy eyeballing Amir and Justina.

"You over there looking like a star too," I finally said, kissing Peaches on the cheek and I wasn't lying, she was a bad bitch. She had a super short haircut that highlighted her striking features. Her skin was so chocolate and smooth; you were tempted to rub your finger across her face to see if she was real.

"So what's going on wit' you?"

"Nothing, getting used to being free…what

about you?"

"Girl, I got used to it real quick. Back in the game making major paper. My people came through for me like they said they would."

"That's what's up. I'm still trying to figure out what I'ma do with my life."

"I told you before I got out that when you beat them charges I wanted you to partner up with me."

"Man, you still on that," I stated raising an eyebrow.

"It ain't changed."

"Why me?"

"I'm doing so much business I need a partner and I don't trust none of these hoes out here. But you…you showed you is a real down ass bitch when we was locked up together."

"I hear you but I dabbled in some illegal shit before I got locked up for that other bullshit and the feds ran up in my man's crib and locked both of our asses up. If it wasn't for my grandfather they would've tried to stick me with some serious charges. I believe my ex is still locked up behind that shit."

"I feel the hesitation but how I run my operation is tight. It's getting too much for me to handle by myself but I don't want that money to stop."

"How much you making?" I couldn't lie Peaches had me curious.

"I'll put it like this. If business keeps booming I'm on my way to be a millionaire."

"Bitch, stop lying."

"I kid not. I got the direct plug that give me bottom basement prices. I deal with the top dudes and they got spots allocated and want to give me more but I'm afraid to say yes because I know I can't handle it and I don't want to take on too much and then fuck up."

"I feel you and I appreciate you thinking of me but I don't think it would be a good move for me. My family would fuckin' flip if they found out."

"They wouldn't have to know."

"Shit I have all that money coming in, I'ma wanna spend it."

"Your people got paper, they'll just think you spending what they got."

"I think I'ma have to pass."

"Girl…"

"Aaliyah, I thought that was you," I heard Amir say interrupting Peaches. I was so engaged in my conversation with Peaches I didn't even notice him walking up and Justina's dumbass had the boldness to be standing right behind him.

"What do you want?"

"I've called you and left a ton of messages but you haven't returned any of my calls. I even came by your house a few times and your mother always says you're not home." I peeped Justina rolling her eyes on the sly.

"Hoe, you begging for a beat down…ain't you," I spit, unable to ignore Justina's presence any longer. "You and your grimy mother still walking around this motherfucker free. So you know, your mother can try to check into as many crazy houses, surround herself with a bunch of attorneys but they'll only be able to keep her out of jail for so long. Then you have the nerves to act like you got amnesia and can't remember who shot you…it was yo' damn mama fool."

"I don't know what you're talking about," Justina had the audacity to say in a little mousey voice.

"Keep playing dumb but you and your mother picked the wrong bitch to fuck with. Both of you are going down and ain't nobody gonna be able to save the two of you."

"Aaliyah, I didn't come over here to get you upset."

"What the fuck did you think was gonna happen bringing that deadly disease over here. It's amazing how you don't have shit to say while you're standing in front of me but had diarrhea of the mouth when yo' lying ass was on the stand. Both of you get the fuck away from my table," I said turning away.

"I'm not giving up on you. I'll keep reaching out to you until we sit down and talk things out." Amir stood there for a few minutes and when he saw that I was finished talking he walked off with Justina.

"Girl, what in the hell was that about?" Peaches questioned after they were gone.

"That conniving hussy is the reason I was locked up for all those months."

"Oh, that's the chick that said you shot her and Sway Stone?"

"Yes, when she knew the whole time it was her crazy ass mother that pulled the trigger."

"What! Her own mother shot her?"

"Yes, but I believe she thought it was me and didn't realize that shit until after the fact. But none of that matters because Justina knew I didn't shoot her but she lied because she wanted to keep me and Amir apart…well the shit worked."

"It seems like dude definitely doesn't want you all to be apart."

"It's too late. I don't understand how he can have any sort of relationship with her after what she did to me," I said, shaking my head.

"Sometimes people don't understand how badly their actions can hurt you."

"Or maybe they just don't care," I sulked. "But fuck them, we have bigger and better things to scheme on like when you want to start this partnership."

"Huh?"

"You heard me. When do you want to start this partnership or have you already changed your mind?"

"Hell no! But I guess you have and I'm glad you did. I'm ready whenever you are."

"Then let's do it!" I knew that I shouldn't go into business with Peaches but I didn't care. I was tired of my mind being suffocated with thoughts of Justina her mother and especially Amir. The pain in my heart from the day he walked out on me when I was in jail was still fresh. I felt that if I didn't create new memories I would be haunted by the old ones for the rest of my life. If going into business with Peaches, even if it was illegal could get my mind off that bullshit then so be it, I was in.

Precious

"What are you doing here?" When I opened the front door I knew that probably wasn't the greeting Lorenzo was expecting but I was surprised to see him.

"Talking to you on the phone wasn't enough for me anymore. I had to see you."

"You shouldn't have come. I thought we agreed that we wouldn't see each other for a while."

"It's been three months. I would call that awhile. Can we talk or are your kids here?"

"No, Xavier is spending the night with his dad and Aaliyah is out with a friend."

"Then can I come in?" I hesitated for a moment but then stepped to the side so Lorenzo could come inside. "You know how much I've missed you."

"I've missed you too," I admitted after closing the door.

"I can't take being away from you. I know I said I could but I was wrong."

"Lorenzo, don't"

"Don't what, tell you the truth. You mean a lot more to me then I wanted to admit."

"Why is that?"

"Why do you mean a lot to me?"

"No, why didn't you want to admit it?"

"Precious, you know both of us came into this with a lot of baggage. You turned to me because you weren't happy in your marriage and I figured you were safe for me because I wouldn't allow myself to catch real feelings for a married woman but I was wrong. After Dior I didn't believe I could ever love another woman again but..." Lorenzo's voice trailed off.

"But what?"

"With you getting a divorce I want us to give this a go."

"I don't know. The complications that come with us being together run so deep."

"Are you saying that what we have for each other isn't strong enough to get us through it?" Before I could answer, Lorenzo was standing over me looking down. The man's eyes always had a way of hypnotizing me, the same way Supreme's used to do. I don't want to be without you," he stated in a low tone before kissing my forehead, then the tip of my nose and finally my lips. I welcomed the warmth of his tongue as I missed it. I missed everything about him from his scent to the embrace of his muscular arms to the way he felt when he was inside of me.

"Don't stop," I sighed when his mouth left mine.

"Are you sure? I don't want to pressure you into doing something you don't want to."

"I want to," I said, taking Lorenzo's hand and leading him upstairs to my bedroom. By the time we got behind closed doors we were practically out of our clothes. Lorenzo lifted me up and wrapped my legs around his back while his tongue made a trail up the center of my stomach until reaching my breast. The moistness of his mouth licked and bit my nipples causing my pussy to drip in anticipation of feeling his dick deep inside of me.

"Damn, I missed this body," Lorenzo moaned as he laid me down on the bed. He then put my legs over his shoulders as his tongue continued to fuck my body. He still remembered the exact spot to lick my clit sending me into an immediate orgasm. He held my arms down so I couldn't fight against the sexual ecstasy that had taken over me. My cries of pleasure echoed throughout the room as Lorenzo gave me exactly what my body craved. Once he slid his dick inside of me my mind was gone. My juices flooded his thick tool which seemed to make his strokes go deeper and deeper.

"You feel so fuckin' good," I purred, wishing I could bottle this sensation and carry it around with me on a daily basis.

"Baby, so do you. I don't ever want to be without this pussy. I want it to belong to me."

"It does," I found myself saying without any uncertainty. As my nails sunk into Lorenzo's skin I couldn't determine if I was in love with him or sprung on the dick, but at this moment it didn't even matter because the shit felt too good for me to care.

"Mom, open the door!"

knock...knock...knock... I heard Aaliyah's voice but I was still halfway sleep. It was like part of my brain was alert but my body was immobile.

"Mom, I have to talk to you!" By the time my brain and my body finally clicked in unison Aaliyah was standing in my bedroom with her mouth wide open in shock. At first I didn't understand why she was looking at me like that until I turned to see

Lorenzo sleeping beside me. *Fuck! I forgot to lock the door. How can I explain this away?* I wondered to myself.

"Aaliyah, let me explain…"

"There is nothing that can explain why you have another man in the bed you shared with my father. How dare you!"

"Aaliyah, calm down."

"What's going on?" hearing Lorenzo's groggy voice made me look away from Aaliyah and turn in his direction. His eyes were closed and you could tell he was struggling to fully wake up.

"You wanna know what the hell is going on? You just fucked my mother in my father's bed! If I had a gun I would shoot you!" That surely woke Lorenzo up quick, fast and in a hurry. He rose up in the bed and witnessed the fucked up predicament we had put ourselves in.

"That's enough! You have every right to be upset but you're totally out of line. I'm your mother, don't forget that!" I was trying my hardest to keep my composure because I wished with everything inside me that Aaliyah had never walked in on us but it was hard because she was such a firecracker just like her father and me.

"You know what, I'm done with you. You've destroyed this family and then you slap us in the face again by bringing that into our house," Aaliyah scolded, flipping her hand up towards Lorenzo. "That motherfucker means that much to you, you all can have each other but I'm outta here!" She screamed, before storming off.

"Aaliyah, comeback here." I jumped out of bed to go after her and realized I was naked. I grabbed Lorenzo's shirt since it was the closest thing within my grasp, chasing after Aaliyah while covering myself up. "Aaliyah, what are you doing?" I wanted to know once I reached her bedroom.

"I'm leaving."

"No you're not," I said taking her clothes out of her suitcase as soon as she put them in.

"I don't need your permission to leave this house, I'm over eighteen. I don't want to be here with you. You disgust me."

"I know you're angry but don't speak to me like that."

"Or what? You're going to put me on punishment…please. I've spent months in prison, there is nothing you can do to me that's worse than that but kill me." It wasn't until that very moment that I fully comprehended the warning from Genesis that day in the restaurant about Aaliyah's time in jail. The daughter I once knew didn't exist she had changed. I no longer knew how to reach her and it was breaking my heart.

"Aaliyah, I'm sorry. Please forgive me," I pleaded sitting down on her bed. I had lost Supreme I didn't want to lose my daughter too.

"I can't stay here. I get out of jail and all I've been dealing with is drama. My grandfather is in a coma that it doesn't look like he's coming out of and my dad hasn't lived in this house not one day since I've been back home. Then Chantal and Justina are still not in jail and I have to run into her with Amir."

"You saw Justina?"

"Yes, last night when I was out to dinner. That's what I came to your room to tell you. But I don't want to talk about them right now. I'm just dealing with so much and catching you in bed with Lorenzo was it for me."

"Aaliyah, I promise if you stay that will never happen again. Lorenzo will never be allowed back in this house. I don't want you to leave."

"It's too late. I don't want to be here but I love you and I'm sorry for what I said to you. I'm in a bad place right now and I need time to myself."

"Where will you go?"

"I don't know yet, but I'll call you. I have to

go."

"Aaliyah," I called out when she was midway down the hallway. At first she kept walking but then she stopped and turned towards me but remained silent. "I love you too."

The tears trickled down my face but I couldn't blame anybody for the fucked up situation I had gotten myself into but me. I stayed in Aaliyah's room for a few more minutes staring at the pink bedspread she loved so much and all her favorite stuffed animals from when she was a little girl that she kept on a bookshelf. She was still my baby and now she was gone.

When I got back to my bedroom, Lorenzo was sitting on the chaise dressed in everything besides the shirt of his I was wearing. "I didn't want to come out and further upset Aaliyah. I felt it was best I stay in here until you told me it was time to leave," Lorenzo explained. I thought he would be a little agitated after the harsh words Aaliyah spit at him but he was surprisingly calm.

"Aaliyah left."

"She'll be back."

"I hope so but I've never seen her this upset before. I really messed up."

"It's my fault. I should've never showed up

here. You told me to stay away but I didn't listen. I came anyway and I feel terrible. With all that Aaliyah has been through these last few months she didn't need this," Lorenzo said, putting his head down. He seemed to be taking it hard and I wasn't expecting that.

"Aaliyah is my daughter and I've failed her. I don't know exactly when it started but it did and I have to find a way to fix it and make it right."

"I agree you do but also give her some space. She seems to have a lot of bottled up anger inside and it's coming to a head. But who can blame her, she spent time in jail for a crime she didn't commit and that's just for starters. It was wrong of me not to take Aaliyah's feelings into consideration. But I missed you and wanted to be with you. In the process I used poor judgment. It won't happen again."

"I wanted you here," I said stroking the side of Lorenzo's face. "I don't regret being with you but it can't happen in this house again. My children think of this as their father's home and I have to respect that."

"You're right. I recently bought a place and you're always welcomed there." I kissed Lorenzo and even after the bullshit I went through with Aaliyah I was ready to slip out of his shirt and have him inside of me again but I refused to give into my lust and temptation.

"Thank you and I will. I do want to see if we can make this work…you know a relationship."

"I know what you mean and I want the same thing but I won't rush you. Your focus right now has to be making sure that your children are good. I'll be here, I'm not going anywhere." Lorenzo unbuttoned his shirt that I was wearing, took it off and then put it on. I hated myself for not wanting to see him go. Everything inside of me wanted to remove his shirt and let us get back in the bed together but I had to have some self-control.

"Thank you for being so understanding. I'll call you later on."

"You do that," he said, giving me a goodbye kiss. "And, Precious, don't be so hard on yourself. You are a good mother but you're also human. I'll talk to you later," he smiled.

I stood in the middle of my bedroom naked and alone. I knew I needed to give Aaliyah some space but I decided to call her cell phone. She didn't answer so I sent her a text message. No matter how much she hated me right now I needed Aaliyah to know that she could always come back home.

Aaliyah

When I left home the only person I could think of calling was Peaches. I didn't want to speak to either of my dads because as pissed as I was with my mother I didn't want them to know what happened. All of our lives was so full of drama there was no reason to bring even more. I was glad that Peaches answered because my first instinct when I got in the car was to call Amir. With all the anger I had towards him I was baffled that he was immediately the person I thought could make it all better. I pushed Amir to the back of my mind when I pulled up to the gated townhouse community Peaches lived at. I pressed in the code she gave me, and the gates opened. I had never been to this part of Teaneck but it was another beautiful area in Bergen County.

"That must be her spot right there," I said out loud noticing her red drop top Benz in the driveway. There was also a white Escalade but I wasn't sure if that was her car too or if she had company, but I would soon find out. When I got to the door I could hear loud talking and tapping of heels coming near. I rang the bell in within a few seconds Peaches had opened it.

"Hey girl!" She beamed, giving me a hug. "Collette, this is Aaliyah, my friend I was telling you about."

"Oh yeah, it's good to finally meet you," she said extending her hand. "Peaches has told me so much about you and what you did for her while you all were locked up."

"Yeah, but I know Peaches would've done the same thing for me."

"True, I would've but you a pit-bull. Looking at you, you would never think. I guess that's how you caught them broads off guard."

"I guess you right," we all laughed.

"Well, it was good meeting you, Aaliyah, and I'm sure we'll see each other again."

"It was good meeting you too." Peaches and I stood outside for a few seconds, watching Collette get in her Escalade before going inside.

"Ummm, you are staying aren't you?"

"Yeah, why you ask that?"

"Where are all your bags?"

"I left them in the car, we can get them later."

"No problem, can I get you something, I mean a drink?"

"No I'm good. I'm loving your crib…it's sick."

"I love it too although it ain't on that estate level you used too."

Maybe not, but at least this is yours. Those cribs I live in don't belong to me."

"I feel you but all that is about to change."

"I hope you're right. Regardless I appreciate you letting me stay with you, especially under the circumstances."

"No doubt. Girl, put that bullshit behind you. We about to be some rich bitches."

"You seem to be doing pretty well for yourself," I stated while my eyes scanned her residence."

"For a young bitch in the game I'm doing pretty well for myself but fuck that we 'bout to do a takeover."

"Peaches, you are so damn crazy," I laughed.

"I'm so damn serious. These two brothers I get my shit from are so deep in the game. They on some top tier shit. They had the Midwest and South on lockdown, now they trying to get the East Coast. They were having some difficulties but things seem to be starting to work in their favor."

"Cool. Well I'm ready to jump in and get my hands dirty and I'm not scared a lick. Hustling is all in my DNA and it goes way back from generations."

"I can tell. You one of those bitches don't nobody ever see coming until it's too late."

"So when do I get started?"

"Those brothers who are technically my boss and now yours since we're partners are having an exclusive, intimate party at their house tomorrow. We're invited."

"Really, sounds interesting."

"It should be. I've never been invited to their crib before so clearly I'm moving up on the totem pole of importance."

"Must be."

"I think tomorrow will be the perfect time to introduce you to them. I already mentioned that I would be bringing my new partner so they're looking forward to meeting you."

"I didn't bring any clothes for a party."

"You can borrow something of mine. We're around the same size."

"Thanks but no thanks, I like to wear my own clothes. Plus I always love an excuse to go shopping. Tomorrow we'll make a day of getting pampered and hitting up some high-end boutiques. I can run up my parent's credit card a few more times."

"Just think, pretty soon you won't even need it. You'll be balling so hard you won't have nothing but endless cash coming out your pockets."

"Cheers to that. Maybe I will have that drink you mentioned." I followed Peaches to the kitchen and she pulled out a cold bottle of champagne and two glasses. I was def in the mood for a little celebrating.

"Here you go," Peaches said handing me a glass of bubbly.

"Cheers to my new beginning and a Boss Bitch in the making." We clanked our glasses and for the first time in what seemed like forever I was optimistic about my life.

"I can't believe how much shit we bought today," I said, dropping my shopping bags in the front door entrance when we got back to Peaches' townhouse.

"Girl, I saw so much hot shit I could've shopped for another few hours. I'm glad you said it was time to go because I was losing my mind in that last store."

"Once I found what I was wearing tonight I was good. It just took about seven stores and endless other outfits for me to figure it out."

"Well we need to hurry up and get ready because we're already running late."

"I'll be ready in less than an hour. But let me go get some champagne first. I can drink it while I'm getting dressed."

"Cool, let's do this."

Luckily Peaches had two full size bathrooms in her crib so we could get ready at the same time. Getting all dolled up for a party was exciting for me, as I hadn't done it in a very long time. The more I thought about it, I realized the last time I did get dressed up for a party was the night of Sway's murder. Even after all this time had passed it was hard to believe that Sway Stone was dead. Although all the charges against me were dropped I would forever be connected to his murder. A few weeks ago VH-1 did a special on him in celebration of his birthday and of course they showed pictures of us together, talked about the charges against me, and my involvement in his death. Of course they waited to the end of the segment to mention those charges were dropped. The sensationalism of it all made for great television but for me it was like a dark cloud hanging over my head. I didn't want my life to be remembered as the girl who was accused of murdering hip-hop mega superstar Sway Stone. I was determined to create a different legacy even if it meant moving kilos.

By the time I finished having flashbacks of my time with Sway I was dressed and ready to go. All I had to do was brush my hair and apply some makeup. My fuchsia Alexander McQueen silk chiffon open back mini dress was so risqué that I opted for a clean look when it came to my face. I went light on the eyes, some bronzer with a dab of Wonderstruck lip-gloss. I felt so fuckin' sexy and I loved it. I grabbed my purse and headed downstairs so we could go.

The drive to our destination seemed rather long but I think it was because I was going to an unfamiliar place. The brothers lived further out in Somerset County in a small city called Bernardsville. I had never been in this part of Jersey but when Peaches turned down Claremont Rd., I felt right at home because there was nothing but money mansions decorating the street. One in particular sitting atop a mountain really caught my eye and of course that ended up being the winding driveway Peaches pulled up to.

"Damn, I knew them niggas was making bank but they gettin' it foreal. Watch we gon' be just like them, Peaches bragged.

"You ain't sayin' nothin' but a thang," I chimed in, cosigning on our dreams of being female drug lords.

"Let's do it!"

When we got to the entrance Peaches showed what I guess was some type of invite to the security guard. The funny part was that the invite was a little black and chrome toy gun that fit in the palm of your hand. It had a serial number engraved in it that matched up with a number on the guest list. The valet took the keys to the car and we headed to the entrance feeling and looking like some bad bitches. When we stepped inside, the spatial design all portrayed the finest materials and craftsmanship, Corinthian columns, Enkeboll moldings, absolute black moldings and Swarovski chandeliers. We could hear two men talking so we followed the voices. When we entered the great room there were about a dozen people sitting down in chairs and another dozen standing up.

They were all listening to the two men speak. They both stopped for a second and stared at us when we came in.

"That's the brothers," Peaches whispered as we took a seat on a couch that wasn't occupied. While listening to the men I couldn't believe that two brothers could look totally different but be equally fine. Both of them had an aura about them that was magnetic. There was one attribute that was a dead giveaway they were related. They shared the exact same smile with a dimple on the left side. After taking in the sexiness of the two brothers I inspected everybody else. It seemed that there were mostly couples in attendance. The men were all dressed in what seemed to be tailored suits but the women had no style at all. It was like they threw on a bunch of expensive name brand shit but knew nothing about fashion. They just wanted to be able to brag and say they man had long money and could afford to buy them such and such labels.

"Come on, I want to introduce you to the brothers," Peaches said, grabbing my arm after they finished talking.

"Girl, you have to give me one second. I need to go to the bathroom. Those few glasses of bubbly I had before we left have kicked in."

"Go 'head, I'll be over there talking to them so just come over."

"Cool." I wanted to run to the bathroom but felt it wouldn't be ladylike so I fast walked instead. "Excuse me, where is the restroom?" I asked, one of the servers who were working the party. She pointed down the hall and I rushed in that direction. Luckily nobody was occupying the bathroom. After I did what I had to do, I washed my hands and checked my appearance in the mirror. I freshened up my face and brushed my hair before making my exit. *Now I'm ready to meet my new bosses* I thought opening the bathroom door.

"Oh shit," I jumped.

"My apologies, I didn't mean to scare you."

"Well, if you're standing directly in front of somebody when they open the door it's bound to scare them." I had to catch myself from going off because after the initial shock wore off I quickly realized that it was one of the brothers who had caught me off guard.

"Again, I apologize."

"Apology accepted, now excuse me."

"Wait, I actually came over here because I wanted to speak to you. You're Aaliyah, correct?"

"Yes, I am."

"Peaches informed me that you had come to the bathroom. I was hoping we could discuss some things in private."

"Some things like what?"

"Come with me into my office," he continued without answering my question. I went ahead and followed him, wondering what the hell he needed to say to me in private. "Close the door," he directed as he made his way behind his opulent marble desk. Inside his office he had shelves and shelves of nothing but books. He also had a huge portrait of himself and his brother along with other paintings that I could tell were very expensive. Nico had become a huge art collector in the last few years so he had already schooled me on deciphering between the good shit and the bullshit.

"So again, what would you like to talk to me about?"

"First, let me introduce myself. I'm Emory, and welcome to my home."

"And a beautiful home it is, thanks for having me."

"You should be more than comfortable; you've grown up in homes like this all your life."

"True, but it doesn't stop my appreciation for them."

"So Aaliyah, Peaches tells me you're her new partner. Why would a young lady like yourself who has access to all the money anybody would ever need want to get involved in this business?"

"That's a fair question, but like I told Peaches, that's not my money. Yes, I've been given everything that I've ever wanted in life, but now I want to be able to give it to myself. Not relying on my parents to do so."

"What about school?"

"What about it?"

"You have no plans to attend college?"

"I did at one time but I'm not sure."

"Why is that?"

"You seem to know a lot about me so I'm sure you're aware that I met Peaches while I was locked up in prison."

"Yes, I know about that."

"Well that experience and a lot of other things have made me rethink what I want to do. Right now I don't want the demands that come with being in school. For almost a year, somebody was telling me exactly what I had to do from when to go to sleep when I had to wake up. I need a break from structure. I want to enjoy my freedom."

"With freedom comes a lot of responsibility.

You do understand that?"

"What's your point?"

"The point is that I don't want some spoiled rich girl who doesn't have a care in the world fuckin' up my organization. My brother and I built this shit from scratch. See unlike you, we weren't born shitting out money; we had to work for it. We both graduated college with degrees in law and business. We took what we were taught in school and applied it to what we learned in the streets. Because of where we came from we were born wanting more but see you've never been hungry and people who've been eating good all their lives make me uneasy."

"I feel you and I'll admit I had my reservations about partnering up with Peaches but I want and need to do this. Honestly, right now I don't have any direction in my life and this will give me purpose." As soon as I said it, I regretted admitting that to Emory. To me it showed how vulnerable I was emotionally right now. From the surprised look on Emory's face I think he was also shocked by my candor.

"I see. Well Peaches believes you'll be an asset to her and this organization. I trust Peaches. She's been a member of our team for a very long time and has proven her loyalty. Everybody needs somebody they believe they can depend on. If Peaches believes you are that person for her then so be it, she has my blessings."

"Thank you."

"But remember, Aaliyah, once you're in, you become a member of our family and loyalty is a must."

"I understand."

"Good, now let me go introduce you to my brother Dale and the rest of the family." For the first time from when he stopped me at the bathroom Emory smiled at me and a sense of relief came over me. This had obviously been a test and it seemed as if I had passed.

Precious

When Genesis called me this morning saying he needed me to come over so we could talk, a million different scenarios raced through my mind. At first I declined and told him it wasn't a good time but he insistcd. So here I was trying to get through the Lincoln Tunnel as I tapped my fingers on the steering wheel thinking about Aaliyah. It had been a month since she left and it seemed she had no intentions of coming back anytime soon. We had spoken on the phone briefly a couple times but we communicated mostly through text, but something was better than nothing.

When I made it to Genesis's place, to my despair as I was going into his building so was Nico. We hadn't spoken or seen each other since a few weeks after Aaliyah got released from jail. Personally, I liked it better that way but I knew sooner or later we were bound to cross paths. Once we got on the elevator I decided to break the silence.

"How have you been?"

"Good and yourself?"

"I'm okay. I'm sure you know by now that Aaliyah moved out."

"What! I had no idea when did this happen?" *Fuck!* I thought to myself. I figured since she told Supreme she mentioned it to Nico.

"About a month ago."

"Is she staying with Supreme?"

"No, she's staying with her friend Peaches in Teaneck."

"Why did she move out?" I decided to give Nico the same reason Aaliyah gave Supreme.

"Her friend is going through a difficult time and Aaliyah wanted to be there for her."

"So is it temporary?"

"Hopefully," I smiled relieved when we reached Genesis's floor and the elevator doors opened. I wasn't in the mood to be interrogated by Nico. If I had known he thought Aaliyah was still living at home I wouldn't of told him otherwise.

"Wow, you both got here at the same time, this worked out good," Genesis said when he opened the door.

"So what was so urgent?" I asked when we got inside.

"Let's go have a seat." When we entered the living room Amir was already in there.

"Hello, Mrs. Mills."

"Hey Amir, how are you?"

"I'm okay. How's Aaliyah?"

"She's still dealing with some things but other than that she's okay."

"I saw her about a month ago."

"She mentioned that to me. She said you were with Justina." My tone was accusatory but there was no since in hiding my disgust for Justina.

"I was but it wasn't what it seemed but Aaliyah wouldn't give me a chance to explain."

"You having dinner with Justina at a restaurant, I think that's pretty self explanatory."

"There is nothing romantic going on between Justina and me but she is going through a tough time. She has nobody and I don't want her to hurt herself so I'm just trying to be a friend."

"Last I checked Justina has a mother and a father and clearly they're very resourceful since Chantal isn't locked up behind bars yet."

"Precious, I understand your frustration but let's discuss what I called you over here for. When we're done you and Amir can finish your conversation. Is that acceptable to you?" Genesis asked, trying to play peacemaker.

"Of course, so what's going on?"

"We're all aware of what happened with Quentin. As you know I'm very close to him, in a lot of ways he's like a father to me and definitely a mentor. Ever since he was shot, I've made it my mission to find out who is responsible for putting him in that coma."

"Does this mean you know who it is?" Nico jumped in and asked.

"Not yet but I've narrowed it down to three different organizations. I also believe the same people who ordered the hit at Nico's house did the hit several months back at the monthly meeting we attended."

"What meeting are you talking about?" I was perplexed at what Genesis was talking about.

"Your boyfriend didn't discuss it with you during pillow talk?" Nico was dying for an opportunity to take a shot at my relationship with Lorenzo but I refused to open myself up to the argument so I simply ignored him.

"Of course, normally I wouldn't discuss business with you, Precious, but in a lot of ways you are family and you're Quentin's daughter. I know what we discuss in this room will stay here."

"Of course," I reassured Genesis.

"We've been submerged in a vicious drug war for some time now. The hit at Nico's house let us know just how deadly it was. Whoever did it is playing for keeps. They have also been very strategic and careful about how they move. So much to the point up until recently I couldn't even narrow down the organizations to the three. But I am getting closer. I don't want to move too fast because I don't want to eliminate the wrong family. But as soon as I get concrete confirmation the entire crew will be wiped out. Nobody will be spared."

"How long do you think it will be before you know for sure?"

"I wish I could say no later than tomorrow but honestly I'm not sure. But for our safety I'm closely monitoring all three families. I want to make sure that what happened to Quentin doesn't happen again. Precious, I've had a couple of men watching your house."

"You have? I had no idea."

"I didn't want to alarm you but I also wanted you to be protected. But to be safe I want to add a couple more to be on your premises."

"You think that's really necessary?"

"I wouldn't be doing it if I didn't think it was. You have ties to Quentin and Nico."

"Don't forget Lorenzo," Nico added.

"The point is you're firmly in the mix, Precious. They can easily make you a target. So until we have this situation under control we all have to watch our back and front."

"I understand. What about Aaliyah?"

"What do you mean? I told you your house is being guarded and whenever you all leave somebody will be following."

"Aaliyah's not staying at home right now."

"Where is she staying?" Amir jolted into the conversation. He had been so quiet once Genesis started talking I almost forgot he was still in the room.

"She's staying with her friend Peaches in Teaneck."

"Do you have the address? I'll get somebody on her."

"Yes, I'll write it down for you. Do you think I should let her know?"

"No, I think Aaliyah should be fine. Nobody knows her whereabouts at her friend's house. But I'll put somebody on her just to be safe. We don't need to bring any unnecessary stress on her, she's been through enough."

"I agree with Genesis. Under the circumstances, staying with a friend might be the best thing for Aaliyah. It'll keep her safe and away from all the bullshit," Nico said.

"Maybe I should let Xavier stay with Supreme or his grandparents for a while until this all blows over."

"That would be a good idea," Genesis agreed.

"Mrs. Mills, if you don't mind I also want the address to where Aaliyah is staying so I can go see her."

"Amir, I don't think that's a good idea. If she's not returning your phone calls then she isn't ready to see you."

"Can you at least tell her that I asked about her?"

"Sure, I can do that."

"Thanks," Amir said, putting his head down. I had to admit I felt somewhat sorry for Amir. He was just a kid and he found himself in the middle of a bad situation. He had known both Aaliyah and Justina practically his entire life, they were all the best of friends until teenage love got in the way and brought out the worse in Justina. Although I had a strong feeling Amir was in love with Aaliyah

I believed he still cared about Justina if only on a friendship level and didn't want to completely abandon her. It was complicated and I wasn't sure when or if it could be worked out in his and Aaliyah's favor.

"I have to be going. I'm stopping by the hospital to visit Quentin."

"Precious, if you don't mind waiting for a few minutes we can go to the hospital together."

"No problem. Take your time." I walked over to the massive window to take in the impressive view of New York City while I waited for Genesis. He and Nico headed towards his office to talk. I thought Amir would go to but instead he came over to speak with me.

"I know it might seem like I'm badgering you but I feel like you're all I have left to plead my case for me to Aaliyah," Amir said, now standing next to me in front of the window.

"Amir, to be honest with you, I don't believe I would be very effective in pleading your case to Aaliyah. We're not on the best of terms right now."

"What happened, if you don't mind me asking?"

"It's a long story. I haven't given up on her but besides the issues Aaliyah has with me she's in an unusual place right now. Spending all those months in jail really did a number on her psyche. I think she needs some space to find herself again."

"I blame myself in so many ways."

"Why?"

"I should've been upfront with Justina about my feelings for Aaliyah before things got out of hand, maybe this all could've been avoided."

"When you're dealing with crazy people the only way things can be avoided is to get rid of them. You had no control over what Chantal did and you had no control over Justina's lies."

"Justina claims that she really didn't know her mother shot her and found out otherwise in court like everybody else. She's adamant that she really thought it was Aaliyah."

"And you believe her?" I could tell Amir was struggling to answer the question.

"I want to believe her. I can't imagine the girl that had been one of my best friends my entire life and was my girlfriend at one time could be that deceitful. She's just not that type of person."

"Amir, sometimes you have to see people for who they are and not for what you want them to be. I knew from the first time I spoke to Justina about that night she was lying. But I have no emotional attachment to her so it was easy for me to see the truth. Your delusions about the role Justina played in all this is going to make it impossible for you to rebuild your friendship with Aaliyah."

"I know I messed things up with Aaliyah. I always knew she was innocent but I did feel guilty about what happened to Justina. I have to make things right. I let Aaliyah down once. I don't want to do it again."

"Put this address in your phone. Hopefully you can convince Aaliyah to let you in when you go see her."

"Thank you so much," Amir said as I gave him the address. "I'ma go try and see her right now. Tell my dad I'll call him later."

"Will do, and good luck." Watching Amir rush out made me think about how beautiful young love is. It had no fear only hope and determination. The older you got the more walls you put up to avoid being hurt."

"Precious, I apologize for taking so long. Are you ready?"

"Sure am."

"Where did Amir go?"

"I gave him the address to where Aaliyah is staying. He went to go see her."

"Good for him. I hope they can work things out. You know I'm very fond of Aaliyah. I think they would be good together."

"I don't. No disrespect, Genesis, I like Amir but my daughter deserves better. She deserves a man that can pick a side and stick to it. As far as I'm concerned he turned his back on Aaliyah and sided with Justina, that's unacceptable."

"Nico, that's not what happened. Amir was always on Aaliyah's side. He loves her very much. He has for a long time and has never stopped. I know this because my son told me."

"He has a strange way of showing it."

"You guys that's enough," I said wanting to put out the fire before it even had a chance to start burning. "Aaliyah and Amir have to figure this out on their own. Whatever decision they make we should support. Now let's go see Quentin."

"Sounds like a plan," Genesis said, picking up his car keys."

"I'll get with you later, Genesis. I'll let you know how this meeting goes."

"Sounds good but call me if you have any problems."

"I guess Nico is still pissed with me," I said to Genesis, after Nico left and didn't even bother saying goodbye to me.

"I told you that Nico would have difficulty dealing with your relationship with Lorenzo."

"I understand that but at some point Nico is going to have to let it go."

"I don't know if he'll be able to do that anytime soon. You're going to have to give Nico time."

"I hear you. Luckily I don't have to deal with him on a daily basis because I wouldn't be able to bite my tongue like I did today. With those slick ass comments he was making to get a rise out of me."

"You did the right thing by playing it cool. "

"Does he know I'm still seeing Lorenzo?"

"I'm sure he has a pretty good idea especially since you and Supreme are separated."

"I don't like to pry into Lorenzo's business affairs but has our relationship affected his dealings with you all?"

"Yes and no. We're all invested in certain businesses together and because there is a lot of money involved nobody wants it fucked up. Before all this happened the three of us would sit down together discuss strategies and how to proceed with new business ventures, now I have to meet with Nico and Lorenzo separately," Genesis explained, while we were leaving out his apartment. "Thankfully they're not letting their differences jeopardize us making money but Nico has made it clear to me he doesn't want to be in the same room with Lorenzo."

"Do you think it'll ever get better?"

"That depends on how long you plan on being with Lorenzo." When Genesis said that the elevator doors had just opened but I didn't move to get on and neither did he. We both seemed to be waiting. I think he was waiting to hear my response and I was waiting for him to clarify his statement.

"What are you trying to say, Genesis?"

"Is this thing with Lorenzo serious? Because if it isn't, the two of you are causing a lot of unnecessary problems and maybe you should both consider ending it before it gets worse."

"I'll keep your advice in mind." This time when the elevator doors opened we got on and we both remained mute the entire ride down. I wondered if Genesis caught the sarcasm in my voice or did it go right over his head. I had a great deal of respect for Genesis but sometimes his attitude reminded me of my favorite soap opera character Victor Newman. Genesis seemed to be diplomatic but his arrogance and need to throw around his authority always had a way of showing its ugly face. But because of his intelligence, charm and undeniable good looks he got away with it. My relationship with Lorenzo did create a sticky situation but at the end of the day it was none of his business whether we stayed together for three months or thirty years. Of course in the mind of the great Genesis his opinion was the only one that mattered. Unfortunately for him, I didn't see it that way. I always walked to my own beat and that wasn't about to change to pacify Genesis Taylor.

Aaliyah

Within a few shorts weeks my new gig was paying off in dividends. I was a natural for this shit. Peaches and I both had our role and we played them well. She was the one that would deal with the brothers and arrange product and the quantity and I was the one that would hit up the blocks and check on the dudes that worked the streets for us to make sure they were on their job. Peaches had no interest in dealing with them but I loved it. In the beginning when I pulled up on them in an all black SUV with jet dark tint and rolled down the back window they were shocked as shit that a bitch was in the ride. At first a couple of them tried me but when they saw I kept an enforcer with me at all times they realized this wasn't a game. Plus I kept them supplied up so soon they all adored me, they was waiting and looked forward to seeing the all black SUV stroll down their block. Watching and maintaining the streets freed up time for Peaches to build new relationships and keep the ones she already had intact. It became clear that just like any other business, who you know and who know you back is essential to building a lucrative drug empire.

"Clavon, this was our last stop, let's head back to my place. We can hit Newark tomorrow," I informed my driver, letting him know I was ready to get out of Camden. Right when I was about to lean back and get comfortable for the lengthy ride to Teaneck I saw that Peaches was calling. "Hey, what's going on?'

"I'm stuck in Philly. I need you to take the meeting with the brothers."

"When is it?

"Like an hour."

"Why you just calling me now?"

"I lost track of time and didn't realize until the last minute I wasn't going to make it back in time."

"Yo, I been on the road all day. I'm not in the mood nor am I prepared for this meeting."

"Aaliyah, all you have to do is go and listen. Come on, that's why we are partners so we can come through for each other. You have to go, this is too important."

"A'ight. I'm on my way now."

"Cool. The business I'm handling here is going to take longer than I thought so I'll be home tomorrow."

"See you then." When I hung up with Peaches I wanted to call her all sorts of names but one thing I learned from my grandfather was that you never let people that work for you see any sort of division within your team. A lot of times if your workers sense discord they may try to step in and divide. So instead I cursed Peaches out in my head. "Clavon, change of plans, we're going to meet the brothers."

From the short time partnering up with Peaches I understood exactly why she wanted a partner. Honestly it wasn't a want it was a necessity for her. Peaches was successful at what she did because she was a people person. She knew how to kiss ass to the right people and enjoyed doing so but the chick was flighty as fuck. It seemed every other day she needed me to step in and handle something for her that she forgot to follow up on. But she fell off extra bad this time because one thing she never missed was her meeting with the brothers. They were our most important connect and for her to turn over this meeting to me at the last minute meant she was really slipping. I had never even attended a business meeting with them before. As a matter of fact the first and only time I had been in their presence was at the party at their house. There was no need because Peaches dealt with them and I spent the majority of my time on the road. Luckily, I always paid attention to every word Peaches said in regards to their dealings even when she thought I wasn't listening. If I hadn't I would've been ill prepared for our meeting.

When we arrived at their estate Clavon pulled into a secret garage entrance. He knew that was the norm when business meetings were taking place, that way if anybody was watching they couldn't see who was coming in or out. When I got to the door a security guard greeted me and I didn't know what to expect. I assumed he was going to lead me inside the house but instead he took me down some stairs that led to a room underground. The room was like a massive studio apartment. The place consisted of nothing but stainless steel, marble and granite. There was even a full sized kitchen. In the middle of the room was a gigantic marble table and several chairs.

"They'll be down in a minute," the security guard informed me. "You can have a seat and of course help yourself to anything you like," he said nodding towards the food and beverages on the kitchen counter. I decided to just pour myself a glass of water and be done with it. While I waited for the brothers to show their faces I thought about Nico and Genesis. I wondered if they had a room like this. If they did I had never seen it but I guess that was the point, to make sure it was a kept secret.

"Where's Peaches?" I heard somebody say, snapping me out of my thoughts. I looked in the direction the voice came from and saw Emory and Dale coming closer. I wasn't sure which one of them asked the question but I guess it didn't matter because I'm sure both wanted to know.

"She got caught up with an important business meeting in Philly and wasn't able to make it back in time."

"What could be more important than us?"

"Nothing is more important. You all are by far our top priority. Unexpected time restraints caused a problem but that's why she has a partner for when these sort of dilemmas present themselves."

"Are you prepared for this meeting?" Dale, the younger brother asked, although there was only a couple of years difference in their ages.

"Of course," I somewhat lied, but they didn't

need to know that. In the back of my mind I was hoping that the brothers had set up whatever business Peaches was taking care of in Philly so they would understand her absence but to my dismay it wasn't.

"Then let's get started," Emory said, sitting down first. "As you know if all goes according to plan we'll be taking over a large section of Queens." I nodded my head yes although that was something Peaches had yet to mention to me.

"Peaches was supposed to discuss with us at this meeting how she planned on moving a new team into that area and who it would consist of." I sat there with a poker face for a second figuring out what the fuck I was about to say. All the listening in the world hadn't prepared me for this question because I hadn't heard nothing about any of it.

"We have a crew in Newark that isn't being utilized to the fullest capacity simply because they have too many members for the amount of business they are getting in that area. The traffic has slowed down by over fifty percent, due to no fault of their own. It's an election year and the area is being heavily patrolled. We have more than enough guys acting as watch out. We can move the extra bodies over to Queens and it won't affect the business in any of our other areas. I would suggest we start moving a couple men at a time that way it won't create any suspicion. By the time other organizations become aware of what's going on the takeover will already be in effect."

I waited for the brothers to respond but they both stared at me without saying a word. Then they glanced at each other as if reading each other's thoughts. I swallowed hard hoping my nervousness wasn't showing. I wanted to squirm in my seat but knew this was a sink or swim situation. The more nervous I got the more pissed I got at Peaches. I felt she had thrown me into the water with sharks without any sort of protection. Choosing to remain calm, I slowly lifted my glass of water and took a sip.

"I guess you weren't lying when you said you were prepared," Emory finally stated.

"That idea works and it works very well," Dale added.

"I know it will," I said confidently, not letting on I was relieved that they were onboard with my idea. When I came up with the suggestion I didn't exactly pull it out of my ass so I wasn't completely surprised they cosigned on it but the brothers were hard to read so it could've gone either way. What did work in my favor was that I was meticulous at what I did and took my position seriously. Most people would've checked those blocks once a week or every other week but I monitored them on a daily basis or every other day. For that reason I knew every face on each team and where we had the flexibility to move them around.

"I believe we'll be ready to start transferring a couple men over at a time in the next couple weeks. So I need for you to start thinking about which men you think should go."

"I think we should start off with our two best men. Reason being is because we're entering new territory and we need our most skilled players. Most of the team members have been working the Newark area for at least two years so they know what to do and how the operation is ran. Our captain will know which lieutenant he wants to bring with him and who is the most proficient to take over their positions."

"I was thinking the same thing," Dale smiled. "You need to start attending these meetings more often. I had no idea you were so astute." I felt myself about to blush by what Dale said. To have the brothers respect my business savvy was the stamp of approval I needed to boost my confidence.

"That would be nice but the streets need me. I wouldn't be able to come up with these ideas if I didn't keep my eyes and ears to the streets."

"That's understandable but at the same time a great mind has to be utilized to its full capability. You have all the traits necessary to become a boss in this business and I want to guide you through it."

Emory and I both stared at Dale. I was stunned by what he said and from the expression on Emory's face he seemed to be too. "I think we've covered all the basis that we need to tonight," Emory stood up abruptly and said.

"There are a couple other things we haven't addressed yet," Dale interjected as if confused by his brother's statement.

"They can wait." Hostility in Emory's voice was evident but instead of backing down Dale continued to push.

"We don't need to wait. Aaliyah is here and we should complete our meeting as planned." The brothers eyed each other like they were preparing for battle.

"I think Emory's right, we can continue this at another time." I was trying to put a halt to what had quickly turned into a hostile atmosphere and I didn't know why.

"That's fine but, Aaliyah I'll be calling you tomorrow. There are some things I want to discuss with you. Will you be available to meet with me say tomorrow around seven pm?"

"Of course, I work for you," I smiled and Dale smiled back. *Are we flirting with each other? I think we are and I like it* I thought to myself.

"Then tomorrow it is."

"Thank you both for your time and I'll see you tomorrow."

"Hold up, I'll have security show you out."

"Thanks but I remember the way out. Both of you have a good night." When I left out I stood by the door so I could hear what they were saying after they thought I was gone.

"What the hell was that about?"

"Excuse me?"

"Stop the bullshit, Dale. You were coming on to her."

"No I wasn't."

"I know you. And you've taken a personal interest in her."

"What if I have? She's part of the family."

"We don't mix business and pleasure. Aaliyah works for us, she's off limits."

"When did that rule become in affect, unless you're trying to apply it because you've taken your own interest in her. The same way you know me, I know you too. The only difference between us Emory is that when I see something I want I have no problem admitting it and doing whatever necessary to get it. You on the other hand have a tendency to over think certain things. Most of the time it works in your favor but sometimes it doesn't."

Before I could hear Emory's response I heard someone coming and I couldn't get caught snooping so I jetted. But my mind was racing at what I had heard. I found Emory and Dale attractive; to think both could be interested in me was a powerful feeling. But I wasn't going to get ahead of myself. They were educated professional drug dealers on the highest level. They were masters at the game of manipulation and no matter which way I preceded I had to always keep that in mind.

When Clavon pulled into the driveway of the townhouse I was anxious to get inside, take a hot shower and go to bed. I had been up since six in the morning and I had another early day tomorrow. My enforcer Tony, walked me to the door as he always did, I was so tired I was tempted to tell him to carry me.

"I'll see you guys here tomorrow about eight," I told Tony when we were halfway to the door. But without warning the next thing I knew he had pulled out two guns and was pointing them at a tall figure that had popped out of nowhere. Right when Tony was about to pull the trigger the figure stepped out of the shadow and into the light. "Don't shoot," I called out. "I know him."

"Are you sure?" Tony asked. I could tell he was ready to be trigger-happy.

"Yes I am," I assured him. "Amir, what are you doing here?"

"I had to see you. I've stopped by here dozens of time but you're never home. So today I decided to wait all day and night hoping I would catch you and I did. Please Aaliyah, before you tell me to leave hear me out."

"I can do that."

"Thank you."

"I'll stay and wait until after he leaves," Tony said playing his enforcer position to the fullest.

"That's okay, Tony, you can go."

"I can't do that. You say you know him but he's not part of the family. He could be up to anything."

"Actually he is family, so you can go. I'll see you in the morning." I could tell Tony didn't want to leave but I made it clear that was exactly what I wanted him to do.

Amir followed me inside and he remained quiet for several minutes. I wasn't sure if he was trying to figure out how to begin our conversation or if he was worried about the direction I would take it in. "I was surprised but pleased that you called us family," Amir finally said.

"If I didn't say that Tony wouldn't have ever left."

"So are you saying you didn't mean it?"

"I don't know Amir, so much has changed."

"I see that. When did you start walking around with an armed guard and why?"

"My dad hired him for me?" I lied.

"Nico?"

"No, Supreme. He was worried about me now that I'm not living at home." I knew not to say Nico because that would be too easy for Amir to verify. Nobody in that camp spoke to Supreme so he was the perfect person to put it on and it was very plausible.

"That's understandable. I was shocked when

your mother told me you had moved out."

"I needed some space. I had a lot of things on my mind and I didn't think I could figure them out staying home. I needed a change."

"So are you enjoying being on your own? This is a nice place."

"I have a roommate but yes I like it. I'm moving out in a couple weeks though."

"Are you moving back home?"

"No, I'm moving into a new condo in Edgewater. It's right on the water and it's beautiful."

"I guess your dad got it for you?"

"Yeah. I told him that it was cool having a roommate but that I preferred to be on my own so he offered to get me a place." That too was a lie. In the short span of time I had partnered up with Peaches, I had made more than enough money to afford my own place. But again Amir didn't need to know all that. He would never be accepting of what my new life entailed so it was better I kept him in the dark about it.

"I'm glad I caught up with you before you moved."

"I'm assuming my mother was the one who gave you my address."

"Yes. She didn't want to at first but I basically

begged her. I've missed you so much that it hurts."

"It can't hurt nearly as much as it did for me when you came and told me you were no longer coming to visit me in jail. Or on the first day of my trial when you sat in court holding Justina's hand."

"I don't know how I can ask you to forgive me for that but I'm hoping you will. I was wrong. I was overwhelmed with guilt because Justina almost died and I blamed myself."

"Blamed yourself for what?"

"For falling in love with you." I had never heard Amir admit that he was in love with me and I wasn't sure how to take it.

"I'm not sure what to say."

"Aaliyah, I made so many mistakes and I used poor judgment in a lot of ways but please believe I love you more than anything. I can't imagine my life without you in it."

"Do you know how long I've waited to hear you say those words to me? I feel like I've loved you all my life. But you hurt me and I don't ever want to feel that sort of pain again."

"Baby, please don't cry," Amir said, wiping away the tears that escaped my eyes. "I love you more than you know," he said, gently kissing me on my lips.

"I love you too," I admitted, kissing him back. One kiss led to another and then another. Soon our hands were interlocked and I was kissing Amir and leading him to my bedroom at the same time.

"I thought about this moment so many times," he said undressing me before laying me down on the bed. "I just want to look at you for a moment. You're so beautiful, Aaliyah.

"I need you to be gentle...I'm still a virgin."

"Are you serious!" Amir's voice echoed so loudly he couldn't even hide his astonishment. "I had already convinced myself you had been with someone else by now and it didn't matter to me because I knew if we ever had a chance to be together we would share something extraordinary. But to hear you tell me you're still a virgin, after everything I put you through I don't even feel worthy to take something so special."

"I want you to. I've always wanted you to be my first and even when I felt betrayed by you that desire never changed I only suppressed it. There is no other man in this world I would want to take my virginity but you."

"Aaliyah, I don't know when you'll be ready but on everything one day you will be my wife. I won't have it any other way."

That night with Amir was the most beautiful day of my life. Each kiss was gentle but meaningful. He made sure his tongue made love to my insides until it was so wet that my sugar walls was ready to take all of him. My body was shivering with anticipation. Each touch made me want Amir more, but he didn't rush Amir took his time. He seduced my body by treating it like the perfect picture he was painting, each stoke was precise and without a mistake.

"I'll love you forever," Amir whispered in my ear before entering inside of me as our mind and body became one.

Precious

"Supreme, hi." I wasn't expecting to see him as I was leaving out the house. "Is everything ok... nothing happened to Xavier did it?" I caught myself becoming panicked.

"Xavier is fine. He's at my parent's house. I came by to see you but it looks like I caught you at a bad time."

"I have to go meet with Quentin's attorney. Maya will be there so I'm not in any rush. Come on in. They can get started without me."

"Are you sure?"

"Positive." When Supreme came inside I noticed that his energy wasn't harsh towards me. It had been a very long time since that was the case. "So what did you want to discuss with me?"

"I have to get back to LA and I wanted Xavier to come live with me there." I felt like the wind had just been knocked out of me. Of all the things I was expecting Supreme to say, that wasn't it."

"You want to take my son away from me?"

"I would never try to take Xavier from you but LA has been where we resided for years. This only became our primary residence because of what happened to Aaliyah. That's behind us now and I need to be able to tend to my business in LA."

"Then you go and leave Xavier here with me."

"Precious, our son has been staying with me for over a month now and you said it would be for the best due to some business dealings Nico was involved in that could possibly put both of your lives in jeopardy. Now you're asking me to leave my son with you when those circumstances haven't changed?"

"I'm not asking you to leave. I want you to stay but I can't make you."

"What do I need to stay here for?"

"If you leave it makes everything so final, as if it's over and we're never getting back together."

"It is over. That's why we're getting a divorce. But we still have to work together and do what's best for our son."

"You're so calm and cordial. I never thought I would like it better when you were disgusted with me. At least then I knew you cared and there was some sort of emotion. You're talking to me now as if I'm just the mother of your children."

"Don't do this, Precious. I have to go but think about what I said. If you agree you can come see Xavier anytime you like and I'll bring him here also. But LA is our home and Xavier wants to go back too. He misses his friends. Think about what will be best for him."

"I'll let you know," I said turning away from Supreme. I couldn't let him see the tears fall down. I wanted him to remember me being strong not broken. When I heard the doors close behind him I cried and didn't stop crying until I had no more tears left.

When I arrived at the attorney's office I was still shaken up from my conversation with Supreme. It took all my strength and a couple glasses of wine for me to make it to this meeting. After Supreme left all I wanted to do was crawl back in bed and be alone. Having to deal with others especially someone that I despised as much as Maya was testing my very last nerve. But Quentin's attorney was adamant that I come so here I was.

"Hello, I'm here to see Mr. Polansky."

"And you?"

"Precious Mills," I said to the receptionist then immediately thinking that I wouldn't be Mrs. Mills much longer. I glanced down at my wedding ring, dreading the day I would have to take it off.

"Yes, Mrs. Mills," the receptionist smiled. "Mr. Polansky is waiting for you in the big conference room. I'll show you the way. We walked down the hall and the room was to the right. From the entrance I could see the frown on Maya's face, as I was an hour late. At first I wasn't going to apologize but I decided to do so out of respect for Quentin's attorney.

"I apologize for being so late, Mr. Polansky but a family emergency came up."

"I hope everything is fine?" he questioned with what seemed like genuine concern.

"Yes, all is well now."

"Wonderful and feel free to call me Robert, ladies now let's get started."

"That would be nice as we do have things to do," Maya snarled.

"I know the two of you might be wondering what this meeting is about," we both nodded our head because I didn't have a clue.

"Two years ago your father had me draw a living will on his behalf. It stipulated what should happen if for some reason he was unable to handle his day-to-day business operations longer than a six-month span. The allotted time has passed and Quentin's living will now be honored."

"I believe Quentin will come out of his coma. Why can't we wait?" Moving forward with his wishes in a living will didn't feel right to me, it was like we were giving up on him.

"Precious, I too hope Quentin regains consciousness and is able to go back to life as he once knew it. But the reason your father created this living will is because there are certain aspects to his business that requires someone overseeing it. If no one is maintaining the day-to-day operations then the business entities can suffer a severe financial backlash."

"It makes perfect sense to me. Besides we don't know what is going to happen to our father, he may never wake up. So let's get to it, what did he say?" Maya cracked as she slit her eyes at me.

"Your father owns a company called QT Holdings. It's comprised of several different businesses, some are much more profitable than others. Your father left strict instructions on who should run it and how."

"Father always discussed business dealings with me so it's a given that he would want me to run his company and I have no problem with that," Maya said with so much arrogance I wanted to smack the snootiness right out of her.

"Maya, your father did leave a business for you to run. He owns an upscale nail and beauty salon on 64th and Madison Ave. that he would like for you to oversee. Here are the keys to the building and some paperwork you need," Mr. Polanksy said handing the materials over to Maya.

"Are you serious?" The smug look on Maya's face had now turned to complete anger and disbelief.

"Yes," Mr. Polansky made clear before turning to me. "Precious, your father has left you in control of QT Holdings. He wanted me to give you this envelope and here are your keys." What Mr. Polansky said stunned me. Based on my relationship with Quentin never did I think he would want me to run his company. Unlike what Maya said, Quentin never discussed his business with me, our conversations primarily centered around Aaliyah and Xavier. This news threw me for a loop.

"This has to be a mistake. My father would

never leave his business in her hands. Precious never treated him right. She's the reason he's in a coma in the first place. She's the reason he's gonna die. And you want to give me some keys to some damn beauty salon…please!" Maya spit throwing the keys in my direction."

"Ouch!" She threw them so fast I didn't have time to move and they hit me right in the middle of my forehead. "You can't possibly be this crazy. Oh, I get it. You think because we're in an attorney's office that you're somehow protected? Wrong bitch!"

"Ladies calm down," Mr. Polansky advised, keeping a diplomatic tone. But it was too late. I crawled across that table so motherfuckin' fast and snatched Maya up by her neck that I had the heifa gasping for air. "You wasn't expecting this when you threw those keys, you stupid hoe!" I roared. Although she could hardly breathe Maya was shaking furiously in her chair trying to escape my grasp. From her erratic movement I lost my balance and fell off the table landing on top of Maya. I no longer had my hands wrapped around her neck and she was fighting to catch her breath. But I wasn't done with her. I yanked her up by the front of her hair and made sure I had a firm hold before using my free hand to swing on her. I kept punching until I saw blood. All this rage I had built up inside for so long was now being unleashed on Maya. I blanked out the only thing occupying my mind was flashes of all the havoc she caused my family. From Aaliyah's kidnapping when she was a baby, being held captive and beaten, her having sex with Supreme and leaving with my husband and child. This bitch was the nightmare that kept on giving and would never go away. All I wanted to do was beat her out of our lives for good. But once again Maya would escape death, because before I could make it lights out for the snake there were like four men pulling me off of her.

While my legs were free and within reach I stomped Maya trying to get in as many licks as possible. "This ain't over, I ain't done wit' you yet," I screamed still in murder mode as the men dragged me out of the room.

"Precious, what are you doing? It would break your father's heart to see his two daughters go at it like this."

"Quentin knows the history between the two of us. I don't know why he would ever have us in the same room anyway. She's poison."

"I had no idea the bad blood ran this deep.

Whatever business needs to be discussed in the future I will make sure I schedule the meetings separately. You can use the bathroom down the hall to straighten up. Here is the keys and envelope. I will call you later to go over some other things. After you go to the bathroom, please leave the building. It's for your own protection and your sister. Now please excuse me I want to make sure everything is being handled correctly in the conference room."

I understood why Mr. Polansky was distressed by what happened but Maya caught me on the wrong day. I came to the meeting in a fucked up mood then she had the audacity to have a temper tantrum like a three-year-old and throw some keys at my head. Given the way I feel about her it was only divine intervention she didn't leave out of here in a body bag. Lord knew the last thing my family needed was for me to spend the rest of my life behind bars fucking around with Maya's dumbass. That didn't mean I wasn't going to put that bitch six feet under it just meant the shit had to be carefully planned out so after her death I could keep living my life. If anything happened to Maya now all eyes would be on me after our altercation today. So patience would now become my best friend.

When I woke up the next morning my hand was throbbing from that ass whooping I put on Maya. But I had no complaints or regrets. I went downstairs to the kitchen, poured me a glass of orange juice and took two Excedrin. While I was making some toast I saw my purse, the mail and envelope I got from the attorney I left on the counter when I got home yesterday. I decided to open the envelope and there was a letter addressed to me written from Quentin. I took a scat at the table and read the letter. I believe I reread it at least ten times. The words Quentin wrote were so heartfelt and it brought tears to my eyes.

I'm so so sorry Quentin. All you ever wanted was my love and I made it almost impossible for you to get it. All the time wasted because of my anger towards you. And right now I need you more than ever. I've lost my husband and I'm losing Aaliyah. You're the only person that could always get through to her. If you were here I know you could make everything right. Please Dear God bring Quentin back to us we need him I need him. I closed my eyes begging the Lord to answer my prayers. But in the meantime I would honor Quentin's entire requests. If he thought I was capable and trusted me enough to run his company then I wouldn't let him down.

At the end of the letter he told me to seek guidance from Genesis when it came to overseeing his business dealings. It would've been easy for Quentin to just turn over his company to Genesis as they were extremely close but this was his way of showing me that in spite of me always pushing him away he wanted to break down those walls and repair our relationship, that's how much he loved me. I wasn't going to waste anytime making him proud. Without a second thought I got on the phone.

"Hi Genesis, this is Precious. I'm calling you from my house phone," I said, knowing he wouldn't recognize the phone number.

"Hello, this must be pretty important for you to be calling me this early in the morning."

"It is. Yesterday I met with Quentin's attorney and he has left me in charge of running his company until he comes out of his coma."

"Really?" I could hear the disbelief in Genesis's voice.

"Yes. In a letter he left for me he also said I should speak with you about running the business. That's why I'm calling."

"I think that's a good idea. When would be good for you?"

"As soon as possible."

"I was hoping you would say that. I'm available now."

"Let me get ready and I'm on my way." I let out a deep sigh when I hung up with Genesis. A sense of nervousness came over me. I had traveled many paths in life but running a company wasn't one of them. I was diving into unknown territory and it was scary and exciting at the same time. Hopefully the degree I earned from the streets would prepare me for this new chapter in my life.

"I'm not going to lie, Precious. I'm in complete shock that Quentin left you in control of his company." Those were the first words out of Genesis's mouth when I entered his penthouse. I don't think he even said hello first.

"Good morning to you too, Genesis. Listen, I know this came out of left field. I was dumbfounded too but clearly my father believes in me."

"Your father? I've never heard you call him that one time. You've always called him Quentin. Surely him leaving you to run his company hasn't magically made him dad."

"I know I was a little hard on him but that

doesn't change the fact that yes he is my father."

"A little hard on him, you never let up. He went out of his way to have a relationship with you and even when you proclaimed you would try, you shut down all his attempts. Most of the time you acted like he had the plague."

"You have to understand. After all the pain Maya caused my family and for him to get her out of jail and keep a relationship with her it was impossible for me to forgive that. He wore blinders when it came to her and I couldn't deal with it."

"I get your issues with Maya and I agree Quentin never wanted to see her for the disturbed woman that she is but she is also his daughter and he has a lot of guilt for not being a part of her life for so many years. All I'm saying is that you shouldn't of been so cold towards him and now he's in a coma," Genesis said, shaking his head. "He's a great man. He deserved more than what you gave him."

"I know this and it's eating me up inside that I wasted so many years being angry at him instead of us creating father and daughter memories together. All I can do now is respect his wishes and show everyone that he made the right choice by selecting me to run his company."

"Then let's get started. Quentin has some legitimate businesses under QT Holdings but it's just a front. He's the head of one of the biggest drug conglomerates on the East Coast. Right before Quentin was shot we got in a huge new supply so we've been good up until about a month ago. Quentin has access to connects that we don't have a way of getting in touch with."

"In the envelope I got from his lawyer there were some documentations but no names or mention of who those connects might be...wait," I paused thinking for a second. "He did leave me a set of keys to his office. I bet the information is in there."

"I'm sure it is. Did you bring that with you?"

"Yes."

"Good, that's where we need to go. We're in the middle of a drug war and our enemies are beginning to see we are vulnerable and have been slowly trying to take over certain lucrative spots. If we don't get a new supply in soon it will be problematic for us to regain our momentum."

"Have you figured out which of the three organizations is responsible for those hits?"

"I believe so and we're planning on making a move very soon. By this time next week if all goes as planned that organization will be completely wiped out."

"That's the sort of news I needed to hear. I want the people who are responsible for putting my father in a coma dead. Not one man should be left standing."

"If I have anything to do with it, there won't. Now let's go to that office. The sooner we get in touch with our connect the sooner we can start back feeding the streets."

As Genesis and I headed out it hit me that just yesterday morning I was crying my heart out because Supreme had made it clear our marriage was over and twenty-four hours later I was now the head of my father's drug empire. I had mixed emotions about the turn of events. I was the mother of a young son and I would never want to do anything to jeopardize his life. But whether I was running Quentin's company or not my affiliation with him and Nico would always put me in harm's way. Danger seemed to follow me my entire life maybe now that I was at the helm I would have more control over me and my family's destiny.

Aaliyah

For the last couple of weeks I had been waking up next to Amir every morning and it had me in complete bliss. Being with him was everything I imagined it to be and more. Our life together was just about perfect. The only problem was that my role in the drug business required me to leave each morning and be gone for the majority of the day. My excuse was that I was going to school and in classes all day. In order not to raise suspicion I went so far as to purchase books and each day Amir would ask how school was and I hated lying to him but the alternative wasn't an option.

"Good morning beautiful," Amir smiled sprinkling my neck with kisses.

"It's always a good morning waking up next to you." I smiled back.

"Let's spend the day together and take advantage of this great weather."

"I would but I have classes."

"You can miss one day of school."

"If I didn't have two tests today I would. But I gotta keep my grades up."

"No doubt and I'm proud of you for taking school so seriously."

"Thanks."

"Since we can't spend the day together let me at least drive you to school."

"You know my father wants security and a driver with me at all times."

"I can protect you," Amir teased rubbing his fingers through my hair and pulling me close for a kiss.

"I know you can but Tony reports everything back to my dad and I don't want him getting upset. I'm about to move into my new place. I don't need any problems. How 'bout we go out to dinner tonight, my treat."

"Deal."

"Perfect and you can pick the spot. Now let me get in the shower can't be late for class."

"How 'bout I join you."

"I thought that was a given," I laughed as Amir swooped me up and carried me into the bathroom.

"Clavon, we have a lot of stops to make but the first one is Newark," I instructed my driver when I got in the car. I looked over at Tony who was rather quiet this morning but I wasn't interested in starting up a conversation with him so I kept silent too.

During the ride I kept smiling thinking about my morning with Amir and us making love in the shower. I was considering asking him to move in with me when I got my new place. I had warmed up to the idea because Peaches had a new boyfriend and was basically staying at his spot so the townhouse had become like our place. It felt natural for us to make it permanent. But I had to figure out how I would be able to keep my involvement in the drug game a secret. I wasn't sure if that was possible but the idea of waking up and going to sleep next to Amir everyday made it worth the try. My daydreaming about domestic life with Amir was interrupted when I heard my cell phone.

"Hey Peaches, what's going on?"

"I need you to make a stop in Patterson."

"I can't. Today I'm swamped. I can't make it over there until tomorrow."

"Word is there are serious problems over

there. The brothers just called me and said they want you to check on it asap."

"Fine. Let me hit Newark and then my next stop will be Patterson."

"Great, I'll let the brothers know." I was a stickler when it came to my schedule and I hated when it was changed. Going to Patterson would push back every other stop and make it almost impossible for me to make dinner with Amir tonight. Now I understood why Nico and Genesis were never able to maintain relationships because being in this business made it unmanageable.

When we made it to the blocks of Newark I rushed through handling business. I was determined to make it home in time to have dinner with Amir. I wanted to defy the odds and maintain both my relationship with Amir and my position in the drug game because I didn't want to give up either. There was no denying I got a rush from living this life, it gave me a high. It was addictive and I had no desire to break the habit.

"Clavon, our next stop is Patterson."

"Patterson it is," Clavon said hitting the gas.

I kept my fingers crossed that all was well in Patterson and whatever problems the brothers heard about there were street rumors or that all issues had now been resolved. I wanted the visit to last all of ten minutes because to stay on schedule that's all I could spare.

When we pulled up to the block it seemed almost deserted. "This is strange, where is everybody?"

"I would like to know the same fuckin' thing," Tony said, speaking up for the first time.

"Hold up, Clavon, drive a little further up. I think I see a few of our guys coming out that project building. Tony, roll down your window and call one of them over here. I need to find out what the hell is going on."

"I'm on it," he said already rolling down the window and sticking out his head. "Yo homie, we need to speak to you."

"Damn, this ain't gon' be no ten minute visit. My day 'bout to be all fucked up," I hissed under my breath, annoyed as fuck. But if I thought shit was going bad it quickly turned worse. Out of nowhere the air was spraying with bullets. The worker who was walking towards the SUV was the first casualty. The other two workers who were posted up behind him pulled out their weapons and began blasting.

"Aaliyah, get down!" Tony belted as he had a

gun in both hands poppin' off.

"Get the fuck outta here," I yelled to Clavon as I ducked down taking cover. I couldn't see shit that was going on all I heard were shots being exchanged. After a few minutes I realized we still weren't moving and I started thinking that maybe Clavon had been shot. I lifted my head up to catch a glimpse of what was going on and to my astonishment Clavon was just chillin'. "Nigga, drive! What you in fuckin' shock! Move this motherfuckin' car!"

"Yeah nigga, move," Tony barked as he re-loaded one of his guns.

Just when I figured shit was as bad as it could get I watched Tony slump over with a bullet to the head. I literally had one second to decide if I wanted to live or die. Survival kicked in and I grabbed the other gun out of Tony's hand and kept pulling the trigger until Clavon sat behind the steering wheel motionless. He had killed Tony and I was next. I quickly slid to the passenger seat and leaned over Clavon's dead body and opened the door. With all my strength I kicked Clavon's body out the SUV and slammed the door before driving off to the sound of bullets still ringing in the air.

'What the fuck just happened!" I yelled

out pressing down the gas pedal even harder. I glanced to the backseat and Tony was slumped to the side with his eyes wide open. "Fuck, I have to get his body out the car. What if a cop pulls me over," I said, talking to myself out loud. I spotted an isolated alleyway and drove into it. I hated to leave him this way but I jumped in the backseat, opened the door and pushed Tony out leaving his dead body there. I sped off and caught a glimpse of myself in the mirror. The eyes of a killer were staring back at me.

When I got home I saw Amir's car was in the driveway. I was glad to know he was there because I wanted him to hold me and tell me everything would be ok but I was also nervous because there was no way I could tell him what I just went through. "Calm down, Aaliyah. You have to relax and pull it together before you go inside," I said, giving myself a pep talk. I got out the car and took my time walking to the front door. I inhaled and exhaled before turning the lock.

"Baby, you made it home early," Amir beamed as soon as I came in. He was sitting on the couch watching television.

"Yeah, I missed you."

"What about your test?"

"I took one this morning and the other one was cancelled because an emergency came up with the professor."

"It's early we can still spend the rest of the day together," Amir said, coming over to give me a kiss.

"That would be wonderful."

"I love how all you have to do is stand here and I get horny. Let's get reacquainted before we head out," Amir suggested caressing my neck. I knew that was his way of saying he wanted to have sex and normally I would be the first one leading him into the bedroom but this wasn't a normal day.

"Let me take a shower first."

"We just took a shower a couple hours ago."

"I know but..."

"Aaliyah, what happened to you?" Amir questioned lifting my chin up, cutting me off mid-sentence.

"What are you talking about?"

"You have blood on your neck."

"I do?" I acted as if I was just as surprised as he was.

"Yes you do. Where did this blood come

from?"

"I have no idea."

"You have blood on your neck and you don't know where it came from. How is that possible?"

Think Aaliyah, think. How can you explain having blood on your neck other than telling the truth that it either came from when Tony's brains were blown out or when you blew out Clavon's brains. But my mind froze. I came up with nada.

"Baby, I don't know where that blood came from. I'm as surprised as you are. It's even more reason why I should go take a shower," I said hurrying off to my bedroom.

"Aaliyah, where are your books?"

"I left them in the car."

"Give me your keys, I'll go get them."

"Why do you want to go get my books?"

"Because I do." There was no way I could let Amir see the inside of the SUV because I hadn't had a chance to clean up the blood splatter.

"You know what, I left them with Tony when I dropped him and Clavon off."

"That was my next question. Why did you drive yourself home?"

"What is up with this interrogation? You're my boyfriend not my father."

"You come home with blood on your neck

that you can't explain and you're questioning me. Cut the bullshit, Aaliyah and tell me what the hell is going on, now!" I wanted to answer Amir but I couldn't think of anything to say that wouldn't make me look like an even bigger liar. "Are you in some sort of trouble? Tell me if you are. Answer me, Aaliyah!" Amir's voice had gotten so loud my hands started shaking.

"No I'm not in any sort of trouble but I think you better go. I can't deal with you when you're upset like this."

"I don't know what's going on with you but trust me I will find out." Without saying another word Amir went into my bedroom, got a few of his belongings and left. I fell down on my bed and kept wondering how my life got fucked up so fast.

Precious

"All seems to be going as planned," Genesis informed Nico and me when we arrived at his place.

"Does that mean you've eliminated the organization that's responsible for the hits?" Nico wanted to know and so did I.

"We've already started and they're dropping like flies."

"We got our new supply in, we're demolishing the enemy. This is a beautiful thing," Nico grinned. "Pretty soon shit will be back running smoothly."

"Precious, you're not saying anything. I thought you would be happy to hear the news."

"I am. I'm just a little preoccupied."

"Is there something wrong?"

"I've been trying to get in touch with Aaliyah and haven't had any luck. I know her and Amir have been spending a great deal of time together, maybe she's caught up in him. She's not really good at calling but normally she'll send me a text. It's making me sorta concerned."

"You should be concerned." We all turned in the same direction and saw Amir standing in the entryway.

"Son, do you know something you need to share with us?"

"I was hoping I could get some more information before bringing this to you but I'm stuck."

"What is it…did something happen to Aaliyah?" I rose up from my chair anxious for Amir to reply.

"A few days ago, Aaliyah came home from school early…"

"Stop right there. School, Aaliyah isn't in school."

"I knew that was a lie!" Amir frowned, while shaking his head. I instantly considered what else Aaliyah had been lying about.

"Continue Amir," Nico said, rubbing his hand over his mouth before resting it under his bottom lip. That's what Nico did when he was about to get extremely angry and wanted to calm down.

"When she came home that day she had blood on her neck and she could not explain how it got there."

"Blood! What did she say?"

"Nothing and then she couldn't explain why her driver and security guard didn't bring her home."

"Aaliyah, has a driver and a security guard. That's news to me."

"She said Supreme hired them because she wasn't living at home anymore and he was concerned for her safety."

"That could very well be true but to be on the safe side let's find out for sure." I couldn't dial Supreme's number fast enough. He answered on the second ring and I wasted no time getting to the point.

"Supreme, did you hire a driver and security guard for Aaliyah?" *Please say yes Supreme.*

"No I didn't, why would you ask me that?"

"Because that's what Aaliyah told Amir. Have you spoken to Aaliyah?"

"Yes, she called me earlier today."

"How did she sound?"

"She sounded good. I told her that you agreed to let me take Xavier back to LA with me and she said she wanted to make sure she saw us before we left."

"Did she say anything else?"

"No. What the hell is going on, Precious!"

"I'm not sure. I haven't spoken to her and

I was concerned." I didn't want to tell Supreme about the blood over the phone because I knew he would've went ballistic. Knowing that he spoke with her today brought me some comfort until I was able to get to the bottom of what was going on with her.

"Like I said she sounded upbeat when I spoke to her but I'll call her and let her know she needs to get in touch with you."

"I appreciate that, thanks," I said hanging up with Supreme. "The good news is that Supreme spoke to Aaliyah today. The bad news is he didn't hire her a driver or a bodyguard. So the question remains is who did hire them and why."

"Genesis, did you ever put one of your men on Aaliyah?"

"We did for a few days to check things out but we deemed it unnecessary. The townhouse she was staying in was a gated community with twenty-four hour security and my men didn't see anybody suspicious following her."

"I need to find out what the hell that girl has gotten herself into. I'm going to that townhouse right now."

"I'm coming with you," Nico said grabbing his car keys.

"I think we should all go," Genesis suggested. "I'll call my driver and tell him to bring the car around.

When we got to Aaliyah's place there was nobody there. There weren't any cars in the driveway and nobody answered the door. Each of us tried calling her on our drive over but she didn't pick up. Then as we were all about to get back in the car my phone rang and it was her.

"Aaliyah, where are you?"

"At home."

"We're at your place right now and you're not here."

"I moved."

"Moved where?"

"To a condo in Edgewater."

"Who got you a condo?"

"Daddy did."

"Oh, the same daddy that got you the driver and bodyguard?"

"If you don't believe me ask him."

"Who got you the driver and bodyguard and why?"

"It's a long story."

"I have plenty of time."

"Well I don't. I only returned your call because daddy said you were worried about me and I wanted you to know that I'm fine."

"You can't be fine. Amir told us that you had blood on your neck."

"I got into a fight with a girl at my job and I didn't want Amir to know."

"What job? You told Amir you were in school."

"I lied. I didn't want him to know that I was working at a strip club."

"What! You're a stripper!"

"No! I said I worked at a strip club. I'm a cocktail waitress."

"You're not even old enough to drink. How did you even get hired?"

"I gave them a fake ID. Now do you understand why I lied to Amir?"

"You still haven't explained why you have the driver and bodyguard."

"They work for the owner of the club. I open up the club in the morning and the owner also has me make a lot of the bank deposits, so for my protection and his, he has his driver and bodyguard take me to and from work. Are you satisfied now?"

"I want to see you today."

"That's not possible."

"Why not?"

"I have to go out of town for a couple of days. I'm actually headed to the airport now."

"Where are you going?"

"Miami."

"What in the hell are you going to Miami for?"

"The owner of the club is opening up a new strip club there and he wants me to manage it for him."

"So now you're planning on moving to Miami?"

"I haven't decided but I am considering it. It won't be ready to open for a few months so I have time to make up my mind."

"Why are you working at a strip club? You don't need any money."

"I want to stop depending on my family and make my own money."

"I hate to burst your bubble, Aaliyah but working as a cocktail waitress at a strip club or even managing one isn't going to afford you the lifestyle you're used to."

"I'll cut back. As long as I'm making my own money so I don't have to rely on you for anything,

I'm good."

"I want you to call me when you get to Miami and I want to see you as soon as you get back."

"No problem, but I have to go now. As you know it's illegal to talk on your cell and drive at the same time. I'll speak to you later."

"What all did she say? All I caught was strip club, Miami...what's going on?"

"Nico, I don't know what is going on with our daughter. She's working at a strip club as a cocktail waitress. She said she got into a fight with a girl there and that's where the blood came from. She also said that the driver and the bodyguard belong to the owner who is her boss."

"So she lied to me because she didn't want me to know she was working at a strip club."

"That's what she said, Amir. It makes sense but something isn't right but I can't put my finger on it."

"I agree with you, Precious." Genesis spoke up, as we all seemed to be analyzing what was going on with Aaliyah.

"Unless she's dating the club's owner. That would make more sense," Amir reasoned. I saw the pain in Amir's eyes when he thought that might be an option.

"I haven't been close to Aaliyah in the last few months but I know how much she cares about you and I can't imagine her seeing someone else while she's with you," I said, trying to reassure Amir but not being certain myself.

"Aaliyah and I had been apart for a very long time before we got together. It would be stupid of me to think that she hadn't met anybody. She could've been seeing him and wasn't ready to break things completely off and didn't know how to tell me."

"You know what, we could sit here all day and try to scrutinize what is going on with Aaliyah and still be wrong. What's important is that we know she's safe and not in any danger. When she gets back from Miami we'll go see her and figure all this shit out," Nico said, getting in the car.

"I think that's a good idea. The most important thing is that Aaliyah is safe. Now that we know she is we can get back to handling our business."

I heard what Genesis was saying and even Nico, but for some reason I wasn't so sure Aaliyah was safe. I couldn't excuse the knot in my gut that wouldn't go away. I wasn't sure if the feeling was me being a paranoid, overprotective mother or if it was something much more alarming. But I grilled

Aaliyah and she had a plausible response albeit not what I wanted to hear but still plausible for every question I threw her way. So either she was telling the truth or my daughter had become a professional liar and if so that was the scariest part of all.

Aaliyah

The sun beamed down on my bikini clad body as I relaxed at what many would call an award winning pool and spa that included an entertainment area complete with a kitchen, custom granite gazebo with hand carved onlays, granite columns and a copper dome. This estate was amazing and the perfect escape. I told my mother I was in Miami but there was no need for me to go that far to get a peace of mind. After that day I was almost killed and I told Amir to leave, I called the brothers to tell them what happened and they graciously invited me to come stay with them for as long as I wanted to. I sipped on my third Bellini wanting to block out everything that happened that day but I couldn't forget. I needed to replay and remember every detail because I was set up and I wanted to know by whom.

"Good afternoon." I slid down my sunglasses so I could see who it was speaking to me.

"Good afternoon to you, Dale."

"Do you mind if I sit down and join you?"

"This is your house. You can sit wherever you like."

"You're a guest here and I don't want to intrude on your space."

"I would love for you to join me, please sit down."

"Thank you. So are you starting to feel any better?"

"Honestly no. I mean being here is definitely making me feel safe and giving me a peace of mind but it doesn't change the fact that I almost died and I had to take somebody else's life so I could live."

"The first person you murder is always the hardest to deal with. There are times I'm still haunted by the face of the first person I killed and all the rest of them I don't even remember."

"How many people have you killed?"

"I've lost count. It's part of the game. I haven't had to kill anybody in years as I have hired help for that but I wouldn't hesitate to do it in a heartbeat if necessary."

"I don't know if I want to become that person."

"Then you're in the wrong business. You never know when you might have to take a motherfucker out."

"I always heard that but experiencing it is something totally different."

"It'll get easier."

"You think so?"

"I know so, you're built for this."

"Why do you say that?"

"Because you're a boss. You're strong you have a lot of heart and you're about your business. You haven't even begun to tap into your strength. But if you let me I'll show you the way."

"You will?"

"Yes, you'll be my protégé. What do you think about that?"

"I like it." One minute I was saying I like it the next minute Dale's tongue was down my throat and I liked that too. I wasn't sure if it was the drinks the ambience or both but soon Dale was between my legs and our bodies were intertwined. Our kisses became longer and more passionate. Then he slid my bikini top up and sucked on my hardened nipples one after the other. I spread my legs further apart wanting to feel him inside of me. When he slipped his finger inside my pussy and began playing with my clit I didn't stop him. Instead I moaned in his ear, waiting for him to replace his finger with his dick.

"We have to stop," he whispered in my ear.

"No, please don't stop. I want you inside of me." And I did. Dale had me overly sexually stimulated and I loved it.

"Are you sure you want this dick?"

"Yessssss," I purred as my voice pleaded for him to satisfy my request. Right when I thought he was going to fill my insides up he stopped and sat up. "What are you doing?"

"Shh," he said putting his finger over my lips. "You're not ready yet."

"Yes, I am. I want you."

"I need you to want me more."

"Huh?"

"Right now you want me sexually but I need you to want me sexually and mentally. In a short period of time you will," he stated confidently, before kissing me on my forehead and walking away.

Dale left me feeling all sorts of hot and bothered and that wasn't cool. There was no way I would be able to spend another minute outside by the pool after what almost happened between us. I grabbed my towel and headed inside the house. When I got to my bedroom I sat down on the plush bed and closed my eyes. My mind was swarming with thoughts, good, bad and ugly. In the last six months my life had had gone in a totally different direction. Although I welcomed a lot of the changes there was still a sense of loneliness but I knew exactly what would make me feel better. I got out of bed and went in the bathroom to take a shower. I was anxious to get to my destination.

When I got to my grandfather's room he was laying there looking so peaceful. He didn't even seem like he was in a coma, more like in a deep sleep. The mood felt serene and calmness came over me. I pulled up a chair and sat right next to him. I held his hand and then I lifted it against my cheek. The warmth comforted me.

"Grandfather, I miss you more than you'll ever know. I need you to come back to me. I feel lost without you." And I did feel lost without him. My grandfather was my heart. He loved me unconditionally. He saw the best in me when there was nothing to be seen. "You're the only person who has always made me feel loved no matter my shortcomings. So many things have happened since the last time I came to visit you. Amir and I decided to give our relationship a try. Things were going great until I got myself in a situation with the business that I'm in.

"Grandfather, I'm not ready to share that part of my life with him or maybe I should. I do love him but I'm so afraid if I let him all the way in, he'll hurt me. I can't take being hurt anymore. But you would always tell me that it was better to have love and lose it then to never experience love at all. I have to give Amir and me a real chance. If you were awake I know that's what you would tell me to do. I'm going to see him right now. I'm going to take a chance and tell him everything that's going on with me. If he truly loves me then he'll accept me for who I am.

"Thank you for listening," I smiled, kissing my grandfather on his hand and then on the side of his face. "When I come back to see you, I'll let you know how everything went. Wish me luck. I love you."

"Isn't this sweet, my father's favorite grandchild, pouring her heart out to him." I didn't even have to turn around to know who the owner of that sarcastic voice was.

"Don't bring your negativity into my grandfather's room. He's resting, respect that."

"He's not resting, he's in a coma. There is a difference. So save the theatrics. My father is completely oblivious to what is being said around him. "

"Maya, don't you have a car to get hit by or a bridge to jump off of? This world has enough miserable bitches to deal with so be gone."

"I think you should be more concerned about yourself, my dear, niece," Maya smirked, before continuing. "It's dangerous out here in these streets, especially when you don't have a grandfather to protect your every move."

"Excuse me. I have important things to do. I don't have time to entertain your bullshit today. But for your own good, you better watch what you say because grandfather hears it all," I winked before leaving to go see Amir.

As I made my way to Amir's place I kept going over everything I would say to him. I kept switching up my speech but one thing remained the same. My opening words would be I love you. If I told Amir that, everything else would fall into place. Practicing my approach made my car ride go by in record time. By the time I parked my car and got out, I was more than ready to confess my undying love to Amir. I missed not being with him and my encounter with Dale earlier today made that even clearer for me. There was no denying I was super attracted to Dale but what Amir and I shared went beyond that. We were lovers and best friends. It was time for me to knock down all my walls and let Amir see me for who I was in its entirety.

I almost felt like running, while walking down the street headed to Amir's building. The sun was out and it was such a beautiful day. Nothing could wipe the smile off I thought but I spoke to soon. "Aaliyah, what are you doing here? I thought you were in Miami."

"So what, you thought Justina could entertain you until I got back?" Here I was rushing to declare my love to Amir and who do I see coming out his building...him and Justina. Now what type of bullshit was that?

"It's not like that."

"Is that your favorite tagline, because every time I catch you with her that's what you say," I said, trying my best not to even acknowledge Justina with face-to-face contact.

"Justina came over to talk to me about something and I was walking her out to her car."

"How gentleman like of you because of course there is no way Justina can manage to walk her ass to her own car."

"Why don't you shut up! I'm surprised you're not doing cartwheels down the street. They placed my mother under arrest today and they aren't even giving her a bond. You finally got what you wanted."

"Nope I didn't. I won't get what I want until you're occupying a jail cell right next to her."

"You really are a bitch!"

"That's boss bitch to you. You don't deserve to even be in my space. And the only reason you are, is because for some fuckin' strange reason, Amir keeps you around," I damn near roared, trying to keep my voice down.

"Aaliyah, calm down. Justina is leaving. Let's go inside so we can talk."

"That's okay. It was a mistake for me to come here. You keep babysitting Justina because I'm done," I said, before running off.

"Aaliyah wait…" I heard Amir calling out but I kept running. I refused to keep playing second fiddle to Justina's phony ass. For some reason Amir kept letting that idiot back into his life but I was starting to question whether he had ever given her up in the first place. She stayed lurking and I didn't need that sorta stress.

When I got back to my car, I slammed the door and put my head down on the steering wheel. Before I had an opportunity to pity myself my cell was going off. I looked down and saw it was Dale. "Hello."

"Where are you?"

"In Manhattan, why?"

"I need you to come to the estate now."

"Is everything ok?"

"Just get here." I ended my call with Dale wondering what the fuck was the emergency. I knew we had a lot going on businesswise but I had never heard that tone of voice from him and I was a bit scared. I glanced up at myself in the mirror, freshened up and hit the road. Bad news kept coming today and it didn't seem like it was going to let up anytime soon.

When I got back to the brother's estate I pulled into the secret garage that lead to the underground room. I noticed that Peaches' car was there. *For Peaches to be here we must be having some sort of*

important meeting. Thank goodness I don't have to deal with the brothers by myself. At least with her here I know I have an ally I thought getting out of my car. Keeping consistent with the routine, the security officer met me at the door and escorted me downstairs.

Dread hit me the moment I stepped foot in the room. I wanted to turn around and run but knew I had no place to go. The energy was off and everybody had the expression of death on their faces. I tried to give a half smile but it felt inappropriate.

"Have a seat," Emory directed, without even looking me directly in the eyes. My throat began throbbing as my air circulation seemed to be getting cut off. I knew it was all psychological but it was distressful all the same.

Emory had me take a seat next to Peaches and directly across from Dale. He also wasn't giving me any eye contact. *Damn this nigga was tonguing me down at the pool only a few hours ago now he won't even crack a smile. Shit must really be about to pop off* I thought thinking of every scenario this could end up being and none of it was good.

"Dale, let me speak with you for a second." Dale got up and he and his brother walked out of the room. I used the opportunity to talk to Peaches.

"What is going on?" I asked Peaches in a low voice.

"I have no idea. Emory called me and said I was needed at the estate immediately."

"That's the same thing Dale told me. He sounded so angry."

"Emory didn't sound angry when he called me but when I got here they definitely weren't happy. They were anxious for you to get here."

"You think they're angry about something I did?"

"Honestly I don't know. We have to wait and see." I felt my hands getting sweaty and it got worse when Dale and Emory came back in the room.

"So what is this about?" Peaches questioned. Her demeanor was relaxed and composed, unlike how I was feeling but hopefully it wasn't evident to the brothers.

"As you both know we had a major hit on our territory in Patterson. It's come to our attention that this was an inside job."

"You mean someone within the organization?" Peaches asked.

"Yes."

"Do you know who?"

"Yes, your partner Aaliyah."

"Me!" I pointed to myself and my eyes darted around the room landing back on Peaches. I was waiting for her to defend me but she was giving me the same eye of death as the brothers. "I don't know where you're getting your information from but I swear I had nothing to do with that hit... nothing!" I barked, standing up pounding my fist on the table.

"Sit down!" Emory barked right back. But I refused to sit down. If the brothers believed I was responsible for that hit I wasn't walking out of this room alive, that I knew. So I had no choice but to stand my ground because this was my life they were playing with.

"I am not sitting down. I had nothing to do with that hit. I had to watch Tony die and kill another man so I could live. That was one of the worse days of my life and you want to accuse me of being responsible for it. What would I gain by setting up that hit?"

"We found out that Supreme isn't your only father. Nico Carter is your biological dad and he's heavy in the game. Maybe you're trying to help him take over that territory."

"Are you crazy! My family doesn't even know I'm in the drug business. They would flip the fuck out. And let's be clear, if my dad did know I was in the game, he would never knowingly put my life in jeopardy for some bullshit blocks in Patterson. My people is rich. And I'm in the game so I can be rich like them too. All this other shit you talkin' 'bout ain't got nothing to do wit' me."

"What do you think, Peaches? You're the one that brought Aaliyah into the fold. As a boss you vouched for her and made her your partner. Do my brother and I have it wrong or is she the snake that we believe her to be?" I wanted to slit Emory's throat for saying that shit. I wasn't anybody's snake. That nigga was treating me like I was some snitching ass bitch or something. But I knew Peaches would step up and set these niggas straight.

"Well…" she paused staring down at the table with her hands folded. "You're right I did vouch for Aaliyah. She showed me she was a standup bitch when we were locked down together. I appreciated that shit and I always will."

"Thank you, Peaches."

"But recently there have been some changes in her behavior. She wasn't even supposed to go to Patterson that day. So I found it strange when I heard what happened."

"Excuse me! You lying bitch! You're the one

who called me and told me to go to Patterson. You said the brothers had called you and wanted me to drop everything and go there. I didn't even want to go to Patterson but you insisted. Now you want to sit here and lie on me?"

"Aaliyah, I don't have a reason to lie. Like Emory said, I was the boss of this and brought you in. All I'm doing is speaking facts. You have changed. I feel like you want me out the way so you can take my spot and have it all." Without saying a word I balled up my fist and swung on Peaches knocking her out the chair. That bitch fell so hard and fast it took her a minute to even understand what the fuck just happened.

"Bitch, you playin' wit' my motherfuckin' life right now." I moved my chair out the way, making my way towards Peaches. "If you think I'ma die based off your lies, bitch you got another thing comin'. I'll beat the truth outta you!" I spit, about to drop another right hook on her dumbass.

"Aaliyah, that's enough," Dale said, putting his hand up. I thought the nigga had loss his voice since he hadn't said shit since I got there.

"Nah, it ain't enough…this bitch lying on me."

"We know."

"What!" These niggas had me confused as fuck. I looked down at Peaches who was still on the floor with her hand over her jaw which I probably broke, that's how hard I punched her ass.

"Stand up, Peaches," Emory said, standing with his arms folded. Peaches got up slowly keeping her calm demeanor intact.

"Emory, I'm not lying," Peaches said, trying to sound like she was the victim.

"Yes the fuck you are!"

"Aaliyah, we got this," Dale jumped in and said. "Peaches, who is Maya?"

"I don't know a Maya."

"Yes you do." Dale opened up a drawer and pulled out an envelope. He then tossed some pictures on the table. "These are five different photos on five different occasions with this woman Maya. You didn't know this but after the Patterson hit we had our people start recording your phone conversations. We know what you did."

"Hold up," I said, picking up one of the pictures. "This my mother's psycho ass sister. What the fuck are you doing wit' her?" Peaches didn't even answer me, instead she started pleading her case to the brothers.

"All that shit wasn't supposed to happen like

that. I would never turn on you guys. Maya just wanted me to set up Aaliyah and she hired me to do so. All those people weren't supposed to die. Maya blindsided me. She said all she wanted was Aaliyah."

"You were setting me up to be killed! You piece of…." Before I could jump on Peaches, Dale grabbed me.

"I told you we got this. We wanted to see how far she would take it and also wanted to make sure you were on the up and up. So relax."

"You guys have to understand, she's not one of us."

"That's where you're wrong…you're not one of us. You shut down part of our territory and caused men to lose their lives all to help an outsider take out one of our own."

"Emory, I swear it wasn't supposed to turn out like that. Clavon fucked up and Maya mislead me. Please believe I'm loyal to both of you."

"You don't know what loyalty means and you know what happens to people we don't trust." Emory pulled out his gun and pointed it to Peaches' head.

"Emory please don't kill me," she begged. "I'll make it up to you. Whatever you want me to do I will but I don't want to die. Pleeaaaaase, don't kill me."

"You know the rules to the game. You have to die."

"That's right, you do have to die, Peaches. But Emory, I think it's only right that you give me the honor of pulling the trigger." All three of them turned to me with shock on their faces.

"Aaliyah, are you sure. I know how it affected you to kill Clavon. You don't have to do this."

"I know but like you told me, Dale, the first person you murder is always the hardest to deal with. All the rest of them you don't even remember, now hand me that gun."

"No…no…no, please don't let her do this!" Peaches got down on her knees and kept pleading with Emory to let her live. But her pleads were useless. Emory handed me his piece, and giving it no further thought I put the tip of the gun to Peaches' head and blasted that ass.

"I told you, you were a boss," Dale smiled.

"You're right. And as a boss my next order of business is to make sure Maya dies a slow and miserable death. She's caused my family enough havoc. I'm going to personally kill Maya myself."

I put the gun down on the table and walked

out so I could go take a shower and wash Peaches' blood and brain splatter off my face. I was quickly learning that you can't trust nobody in this business, not even your so called friends. Everyone was your enemy until they proved otherwise. I chose to be in this game and I planned on winning. So tonight I would rest and get my mind ready for war because now I was the boss and it was on and poppin' and Maya would be the first on my list to fall.

A KING PRODUCTION
I'm Gettin' That
Helicopter Money...
Bad
Bitch
JOY DEJA KING

A KING PRODUCTION

Still The Baddest Bitch

A Novel

JOY DEJA KING

Power

NO ONE MAN SHOULD HAVE ALL THAT POWER...BUT THERE WERE TWO

JOY DEJA KING

Chapter 1

Underground King

Alex stepped into his attorney's office to discuss what his number one priority always was: business. When he sat down, their eyes locked and there was complete silence for the first few seconds. This was Alex's way of setting the tone of the meeting. His silence spoke volumes. This might've been his attorney's office, but he was the head nigga in charge, and nothing got started until he decided it was time to speak. Alex felt this approach was necessary. You see, after all these years of them doing business, attorney George Lofton still wasn't used to dealing with a man like Alex: a dirt-poor kid who could've easily died in the projects he was born in, but instead had made millions. It wasn't done the ski mask way, but it was still illegal.

They'd first met when Alex was a sixteen-year-old kid growing up in TechWood Homes, a housing project in Atlanta. Alex and his best friend, Deion, had been arrested, because the principal found 32 crack vials in Alex's book bag. Another kid had tipped the principal off and the principal subsequently called the police. Alex and Deion were arrested and suspended from school. His mother called George, who had the charges against them dismissed, and they were allowed to go back to school. That wasn't the last time he would use George. He was arrested at twenty-two for attempted murder and for trafficking cocaine a year later. Alex was acquitted on both charges. George Lofton later became known as the best trial attorney in Atlanta, but Alex had also become the best at what he did, and since it was Alex's money that kept Mr. Lofton in designer suits, million dollar homes, and foreign cars, he believed he called the shots, and dared his attorney to tell him otherwise.

Alex noticed that what seemed like a long period of silence made Mr. Lofton feel uncomfortable, which he liked. Out of habit, in order to camouflage the discomfort, his attorney always kept bottled water within arm's reach. He would cough, take a swig, and lean back in his chair, raising his eyebrows a little, trying to give a look of certainty, though he wasn't completely confident at all in Alex's presence. The reason was because Alex did what many had thought would be impossible, especially men like George Lofton. He had gone from a knucklehead, low-level drug dealer to an underground king and an unstoppable, respected criminal boss.

Before finally speaking, Alex gave an intense stare into George Lofton's piercing eyes. They were not only the bluest he had ever seen, but also some of the most calculating. The latter is what Alex found so compelling. A calculating attorney working on his behalf could almost guarantee a get out of jail free card for the duration of his criminal career.

"Have you thought over what we briefly discussed the other day?" Alex asked his attorney, finally breaking the silence.

"Yes, I have, but I want to make sure I understand you correctly. You want to give me six hundred thousand to represent you or your friend, Deion, if you are ever arrested and have to stand trial again in the future?"

Alex assumed he had already made himself clear, based on their previous conversations, and was annoyed by what he now considered a repetitive question. "George, you know I don't like repeating myself. That's exactly what I'm saying. Are we clear?"

"So, this is an unofficial retainer."

"Yes, you can call it that."

George stood and closed the blinds, then walked over to the door that led to the reception area. He turned the deadbolt, so they wouldn't be disturbed. George sat back behind the desk. "You know that if you and your friend Deion are ever on the same case, that I can't represent the both of you."

"I know that."

"So, what do you propose I do if that was ever to happen?"

"You would get him the next best attorney in Atlanta," Alex said, without hesitation. Deion was Alex's best friend—had been since the first grade. They were now business partners, but the core of their bond was built on that friendship, and because of that, Alex would always look out for Deion's best interest.

"That's all I need to know."

Alex clasped his hands and stared at the ceiling for a moment, thinking that maybe it was a bad idea bringing the money to George. Maybe he should have just put it somewhere safe, only known to him and his mom. He quickly dismissed his concerns.

"Okay. Where's the money?" Alex presented George with two leather briefcases. He opened the first one and was glad to see that it was all hundred-dollar bills. When he closed the briefcase he asked, "There is no need to count this, is there?"

"You can count it, if you want, but it's all there."

George took another swig of water. The cash made him nervous. He planned to take it directly to one of his bank safe deposit boxes. The two men stood. Alex was a foot taller than George: he had flawless mahogany skin—a deep brown with a bit of a red tint, broad shoulders, very large hands, and a goatee. He was a man's man. With such a powerful physical appearance, Alex kept his style very low-key. His only display of wealth was a pricey diamond watch that his best friend and partner, Deion, had bought him for his birthday.

"I'll take good care of this, and you," his attorney said, extending his hand to Alex.

"With this type of money, I know you will," Alex stated without flinching. Alex gave one last lingering stare into his attorney's piercing eyes. "We do have a clear understanding...correct?"

"Of course. I've never let you down and I never will. That, I promise you." The men shook hands and Alex made his exit, with the same coolness as his entrance.

　　With Alex embarking on a new, potentially dangerous business venture, he wanted to make sure that he had all his bases covered. The higher up he seemed to go on the totem pole, the costlier his problems became, but Alex welcomed new challenges, because he had no intention of ever being a nickel and dime nigga again.

Order Form

A King Production
P.O. Box 912
Collierville, TN 38027
www.joydejaking.com
www.twitter.com/joydejaking

Name: _____

Address: _____

City/State: _____

Zip: _____

QUANTITY	TITLES	PRICE	TOTAL
_____	Bitch	$15.00	_____
_____	Bitch Reloaded	$15.00	_____
_____	The Bitch Is Back	$15.00	_____

Sh   ooks add

T   rnment
issue   ivered